PERILS OF

"I will take y...
Dorne promis........ .... a production
of *Romeo and Juliet* for you. Get your cloak, girl,
and let us be off."

Arabella regarded him incredulously. "I cannot
come with you, my lord." Much to her
annoyance, her voice quavered where it ought
to have commanded.

He grasped her arm tightly, hurtfully. "You are
an impudent littly doxy. As I have said, you are
extremely gifted, but show me the actress who
will not sell her services. . . ."

"I am that actress," she said. "Now let me go."

His hurtful hold remained on her arm. "In due
time, my love, but first . . . this night belongs to
me, or rather, to *us*. . . ."

The
Player Knight

Ellen Fitzgerald

A SIGNET BOOK

NEW AMERICAN LIBRARY

A DIVISION OF PENGUIN BOOKS USA INC.

SIGNET, SIGNET CLASSIC, MENTOR, ONYX, PLUME, MERI-
DIAN and NAL BOOKS are published by New American
Library, a division of Penguin Books USA Inc.,
1633 Broadway, New York, New York 10019

First Printing, July, 1989

1 2 3 4 5 6 7 8 9

PRINTED IN THE UNITED STATES OF AMERICA

Prologue

The sound of applause, intermingled with childish giggles, followed Petruchio and Katharina off the stage, bringing them back for two more bows, the Petruchio bowing to the audience and then to Katharina, a dark-haired beauty who acknowledged the vigorous clapping with a fixed smile. The Petruchio, receiving a much more enthusiastic response, grinned broadly and bowed gracefully. Then, he seized Katharina's hand and hurried her off the stage.

"I will not go out again," the Katharina said edgily when he would have thrust her out before the curtain again. "You must take a solo bow."

"Not without you, my lady fair," the Petruchio said gallantly.

"Well"—the Katharina tossed her head saying with a pout—"I am not going. They want you, Arabella. They always do. It is the same story every Friday."

"They shan't have me, Serena." Arabella dropped her manly attitude and her deep voice. "Let us change, then. Bettina and Caroline are ready to do the balcony scene . . . Oh, dear, I cannot bear to think of your leaving, and this very afternoon. I am truly devastated—ouch!" She winced as she yanked off her beard and mustache, rubbing her suddenly tender upper lip and chin with a soothing finger.

Serena Sadlier, removing her headdress and the patches of red hair she had left show at her forehead and the sides of her face rather than her own blue-black curls, said, "If you had painted rather than glued it on, you would not be so uncomfortable."

Arabella, removing her hat and shaking out her bronze-gold curls, said, "It would not have looked right."

"Everyone else in school paints their beards on."

"I would not have felt like Petruchio with a painted beard," Arabella said stubbornly. She removed her jerkin and her pantaloons and hastily slipped into her gown. "I notice that you pinned on false curls for Kate."

"They were easy enough to pin. I would not have pasted them on, certainly."

"I have a strong feeling that you will never be an actress," Arabella said teasingly.

"No," Serena said bitterly, "I will probably have to be a governess."

Arabella giggled. "I would not hire you as my governess, were I mistress of a house. You are far too beautiful."

Serena shivered. "Do not say that," she begged. "I will have to find some manner of employment. I cannot . . . I will not be a lady's maid or . . ."

Arabella regarded her with horror. "No, of course, you cannot take such a position. That would be unthinkable."

"And," Serena sighed, "I could not be an actress."

"No, of course not," Arabella agreed hastily and as hastily added, "I mean, you could not possibly enter that profession."

"You mean"—Serena pouted—"that the profession would not have me."

"Of course, I do not mean that, silly." Arabella frowned. "You know what is thought about actors. It is a despised profession, though I do not know why . . . since it would be lovely to act, at least I think so."

"Girls." Mrs. Ormsby, the elocution teacher at Mrs. Pritchard's School for Young Ladies, descended on them. "Before the next scene begins, I do want to tell you, my dearest Arabella, that you were a fine Petruchio, and Serena," she hesitated, "you did very well as Kate, dear." Before Serena could respond, she added, "I am sorry you are leaving us. And very soon, is it not?"

"Papa will be calling for me in an hour's time," Serena said wryly.

"Well . . ." Mrs. Ormsby hesitated and then said briskly, "We will miss you, my dear. And be of good cheer. It may be all for the best, you never know."

"How can it be for the best," Arabella demanded angrily, disliking Mrs. Ormsby's platitudinous comments. "School will not be the same without Serena."

"It is a pity," the teacher said, "but on occasion, these happenings work out in ways we do not understand at the time, and we may be the better for them." A shade passed over her face. She paused and then said brightly, "And one does learn to cope with changes. Still, I must not keep you, must I? My good wishes wherever you go, Serena dear."

"I do thank you, Mrs. Ormsby," Serena returned. "And I do wish you to know that I have enjoyed your classes above all others."

"And we have enjoyed you, too, my dear." The teacher smiled and turned to Arabella. "Are you coming into the audience with me, child?"

"No, I am going to see Serena off, if you do not mind." Arabella blinked threatening tears away.

"As you choose, then, my dear. 'Parting is such sweet sorrow.' I am sure." The teacher hurried away.

"It is not *sweet* sorrow. It is ghastly sorrow, it is terrible sorrow," Arabella cried resentfully. "Oh, Serena, Serena, whatever will I do when you are gone. It will not be the same. I shall pine away like a . . . a rose touched by frost."

"You will not!" Serena managed a watery chuckle. "You will see. Come, my dear, I must finish packing."

In a matter of minutes, the two friends had left the schoolroom. They went through a maze of classrooms and in a few moments they were hurrying up the stairs into a long corridor lined by the small chambers where the boarders stayed.

Serena, who had the room next to that of her best friend, came inside and looked around her. "I cannot believe that I will never see this horrid place again."

"Horrid?" Arabella looked woefully at the open trunks, nearly all packed now save for a pile of garments on the bed. "I do not think it is horrid. It is beautiful because you have lived here."

Serena laughed but sobered quickly. "Your room is much nicer. You have a window as behooves the only daughter of Lord Ashmore, nabob of India."

"Oh, I beg you will not tease me about that," Arabella protested. "Papa is not a nabob. He is an importer and he is also the black sheep of the family because he is in trade."

"I wish my father had been in trade instead of making all those horrid speculations that have landed my brother, my mama, and me in the basket." Serena frowned.

"Anyone can make unwise investments," Arabella pointed out. "I wish it were not your father who had so done . . . Oh, Serena, if only school were at an end, you could come home with me. Papa will be returning from India within a year's time. I wish it were sooner. I know he would want you to stay with us."

Serena drew herself up. She said proudly, "Even if he were expected sooner, I would not come home with you. I am not one for taking charity and besides—!"

"Charity!" Arabella interrupted, glaring at her friend. "How can you even breathe such a horrid word? You know I am not offering you charity. I want you to come home with me because you are my very best friend in all the world. And I would tell Papa that I needed a companion."

"And what would your Aunt Olivia say to that? She does not like me," Serena countered.

"She does . . . she is just—"

"She is not just anything," Serena interrupted. "She does not like me, but we will not dwell on that. I am leaving very soon now."

"I know, I know, and I am entirely devastated." Arabella hugged Serena. "Oh, dear." She raised green eyes grown misty with tears. "Nothing will ever be the same with you gone."

"It will be entirely the same for you Arabella, you will go on being very popular as I have never been," Serena commented wryly. "And had you not taken me up, I would be a rank outsider still. I am a very lesser member of the *ton*, through Mama, who married beneath her."

"I beg you will not spout such nonsense," Arabella said crossly.

"It is true," Serena sighed. "Papa was Mama's tutor and her family cast her off completely for eloping with him. Unfortunately, the scandal is not unknown, as you found out when I came here and Mary Sedley told everyone."

"Mary was jealous of you—is jealous of you, and you are the most beautiful girl in the school and that is no more than the truth!"

"That is pure nonsense," Serena said with a quick glance in the mirror. "You are thought to be the most beautiful . . . Anyhow, my beauty will serve me very little, since now I will have no portion. As I have told you, I shall have to become a governess."

"Nonsense! Some gentleman will surely offer for you, some handsome gentleman who is rich enough to want so lovely a lady at the head of his table—portion or no portion."

Serena said bitterly, "You forget that *I* will not be meeting such gentlemen. We are going to horrid lodgings in Chelsea, which is a great distance from St. James's Square, I can tell you. My papa is not an earl . . . But enough, I must finish packing."

"And you will take this necklace and, when you wear it, think of me." Arabella thrust a necklace of gold and cameos into Serena's hands. "I wish I had my emerald necklace here, I would give that to you, also."

"And I would not take it. Emeralds are for you with your green eyes and they are far too costly to give away and so are these cameos."

"I want you to have them." Arabella's eyes were filled with tears. "Please take them."

"Very well. I do thank you, Arabella." Serena put the necklace into her reticule. "There is no one more generous than you—in the whole world."

A knock on the door caused both girls to stiffen.

"Oh, dear, the man for the trunk," Serena sighed. "Papa will be below, then."

"He is too soon, surely."

"No, he is on time."

"Oh," Arabella groaned. "If only I might leave with you."

"You will be away in another year." Serena flung her cloak about her. Then she moved to Arabella, hugging her, an unusual gesture, for she had never been demonstrative. "Fare you well, my dear."

"You must write. Promise me that you will write, Serena," Arabella cried as she opened the door for Matt, the handyman.

A short, squat youth, he fastened resentful brown eyes on Serena. "You was that slow about it miss," he mumbled.

"Oh, Matt, do not be so mean!" Arabella said reproachfully. "Serena is leaving."

"Aye, 'er father's below'n in an 'urry," he grumbled as he slammed down the lid of the trunk, and hoisting it on one shoulder, he stamped out of the chamber muttering angrily to himself.

"Oh, Serena, if only you were not leaving . . . Whatever will I do without you? I shall be so terribly, terribly lonely," Arabella cried.

"It will not be easy for me, either," Serena sighed. "I wish I did not have to bid you farewell, my dearest."

"Oh, so do I, a thousand, thousand times," Arabella said passionately. She added, "And remember, you did promise to write."

"You have reminded me of that before and I have assured you that I will." Tears gleamed in Serena's dark eyes. "We will never, never lose touch with each other." She embraced Arabella quickly and hurried out.

Arabella was not permitted to accompany Serena to the waiting coach. Instead, she stood at her window, tears blurring the scene in the courtyard below as Serena was helped by a tall, thin, shabbily dressed gentleman into a battered old coach. Immediately she was inside, she leaned out of the window, looking up at Arabella and waving. Arabella waved back and continued waving until the coach vanished around a bend in the road. Then, she went to her own room, threw herself down on the bed, and stared up at the ceiling and wondered what she would do without Serena during all the weary months that must stretch between now and her own departure from the school at the end of the coming year?

"But, of course, she will write and I will write," she told herself, and was distressed at a nagging little doubt in the back of her mind.

Serena, she knew, felt the change in her circumstances very keenly. She had always believed that the girls at school, and their teachers as well, looked down on her because of the scandal connected with her parents' Gretna Green elopement and her mother's subsequent expulsion from the polite world. She had often said very bitterly, "Mama exchanged respectability for love, and I cannot believe that she profited by its loss."

If there were anything that poor Serena wanted in the whole world, it was to be respectably situated, which meant the good marriage that she had hoped to make and that, through her unworldly father's unwise speculations, she now believed forever denied to her.

It was possible that out of an overdeveloped sense

of pride, Serena would cut herself off from all she had
known.

"Including me?" Arabella murmured, and wished
strongly that she were not so certain of the answer.
But they could not lose touch with each other, she
tried to reassure herself. They had been far too close
for that, and Serena would write. She had promised
that she would write—she had promised faithfully,
and such a promise was sacred!

1

Lady Olivia Ashmore was, to her mind, right-eously incensed. The look she visited on her niece's face was grim. "You found out merely by accident," she snapped. "If your friend Camilla Deering had not sent you that clipping from Brighton, you'd have been none the wiser," she said coldly. "And with your father home no more than a fortnight, it would seem to me that you could show more consideration for him. He has been overland and on shipboard and overland again—without a decent rest in months. He ought not to be rushed into another journey . . . and all the way to Brighton, too!"

Arabella met her aunt's gray-green gaze defiantly. "Papa told me that he has always enjoyed Brighton and that he would be pleased to visit it again. He has also told me that he would enjoy meeting Serena—since I have always spoken about her so highly."

"He will do anything to please *you*, but why you want to inflict that wretched girl on him—on us! I cannot understand you, I really cannot. I certainly do not want to have her running in and out of our lodgings in Brighton."

"She is not wretched," Arabella said indignantly. "You have never liked her, and for reasons that are certainly not her fault. I cannot imagine why people keep referring back to that old, that ancient scandal. There have been many since, and considerably worse than an elopment with a tutor.''

''A lowborn tutor who went through the money his wife's family most generously settled on her, considering that she had disgraced herself and them with her actions.''

''And in your estimation, the 'sins of the father' must needs be visited upon the children in true biblical fashion?''

''Let us not talk about sins, pray,'' Lady Olivia snapped. ''Rather let us talk about bad character. That can be inherited, and to my mind it was. You were very close with Serena Sadlier. She came home with you quite often to partake of our hospitality, to be driven about to assemblies, to receive sundry presents. Then she left school a year ago last March. It is now June . . . June and fifteen months later, and have you had so much as a single line from her in all that time? No! The letter you received last week was in answer to your own!''

''She has had a dreadfully difficult time of it, poor girl. She has moved around a great deal. She explained all that in her letter, Aunt, and it *was* a very long letter.''

''In answer to the one you wrote after Camilla gave you her direction, I repeat.''

''She has had difficulties,'' Arabella repeated. ''If I had endured some of the indignities she has suffered, I do not think I would want to write to anyone, either. Poor Serena has an utter passion for respectability.''

''Yes, many of her class do.''

''Her class . . . she comes from a good family. Her mother—''

"Her father was the son of a coal merchant," Lady Olivia interrupted.

"He had an excellent education, which he earned because of his brilliance in school and because his teacher took an interest in him. . . . He did attend Oxford."

"It is a pity he did not learn to save his money. But all that is past history. I am sorry that his daughter must suffer for his errors; she does have a nice appearance and she speaks well, but I feel that she is untrustworthy."

"How can you say that?"

"I can say it because you did not hear from her, in spite of all her fine promises—"

"I read you parts of her letter," Arabella interrupted. "If *I* had had to go knocking on door after door in search of employment and being refused and then getting a position and being blamed because her employer's husband tried to have his way with her . . . I knew she could never be a governess. I am delighted that she has found a position in an acting company."

"I would have said that she could never be an actress, either," Lady Olivia said tartly. "I have heard her read lines when she was rehearsing with you for one of those school recitals. She had no more expression than a waxwork—I am speaking about both face and voice."

"That was two years ago," Arabella said defensively. "If she is employed as an actress, she must have improved."

"And if she is employed as an actress, you should not be seeking her out. Actors," Lady Olivia sniffed. "A raggle-taggle lot, indeed."

"I wish I might have been an actress," Arabella said defiantly. "I love to act."

"You do have a certain talent, my dear. You read well, but compared to a professional . . ."

"I know, Aunt," Arabella sighed.

Lady Olivia said earnestly, "I wish you were married. There have been so many young men offering for you since you came out, and you are nearly six months past the age of eighteen. Lord Kinnard—"

"I beg you will not mention Lord Kinnard," Arabella groaned.

"I know you are not fond of him, child. I cannot say that I myself like him, either—but he does come from an excellent family and he is very rich."

"You could have married Lord Langley, Papa once told me. He said you refused him, even though your only other alternative was to become a governess."

"I was very young in those days and . . . But we are not talking about me. There are other gentlemen who will offer for you, that goes without saying, and it were better you remained in London."

Arabella regarded her aunt curiously. "You are very lovely, Aunt Olivia, and you are not yet in your middle thirties. Why cannot you concentrate on your own possible marriage now that Papa is rich again and can provide you with a dowry?"

"That is nonsense," Lady Olivia exclaimed. "The gentleman who would want to marry a woman of thirty-three would either have his pockets to let or be looking for a second wife to cherish a brood of motherless children and I—"

"I suspect you of wanting to marry for love or not at all. You are always reading romances, Aunt."

"Nonsense, I am entirely happy keeping house for your father."

"Supposing Papa decides to marry again. Indeed, I cannot imagine why he has not. He is so very handsome and he cannot be much older than you."

"He can give me six years," Lady Olivia said. "I wish he would find someone else, my dear. It is just that he loved your mother so wholly, and poor child, she lived such a short time . . . But enough, that is not your concern—nor mine, not at present."

"No, it is not. Aunt Olivia, I want to go to Brighton and see Serena as Maria in *School for Scandal*. You have always liked the sea and Papa has assured me that he wants to renew acquaintances with the town. I beg you will not discourage him."

"Is he aware that Serena is an actress?" Lady Olivia demanded.

"Of course he knows, and *he* does not mind."

Lord Ashmore, subsequently approached on this subject by his sister, really did not appear to mind. "It is little enough I can do for Arabella, and if it will make her happy to see her friend again . . ."

"A friend who is also an actress?" Lady Olivia questioned crossly.

"My dear, they are not all cut to measure. This particular actress went to school with my daughter, and from what I can understand, she suffered severe reverses in fortune that drove her to the stage. You and I are not unacquainted with severe reverses in fortune. And they are very good friends. You yourself have told me that Arabella is discerning, something with which I have come to concur. Consequently, I am sure she would not choose a mere nobody for her friend."

"I must beg to differ with you." Lady Olivia

frowned. "You have not been upward of two to three months in any given year. You hardly know your daughter and I tell you that she has been well-nigh mesmerized by Serena . . . and that chit did not write to her, not a line after she left school, for all they were such great friends and she was often our guest."

"My dearest," Lord Ashmore said gently, "is your memory so short that you cannot remember the struggle we had after Father died—and you went out to work as a governess? If I had not had the connection that brought me to India, I might have been languishing in debtor's prison yet. And who knows what might have happened to poor little Serena. I am sure that you remember that neither of us made an effort to communicate with our friends."

"We might have suffered similar problems," Lady Olivia said, "but still I hated to see poor Arabella so cast down as the months passed and she did not receive so much as a line of greeting from her dearest friend."

"I cannot like that myself," he admitted. "Still, I repeat that we do not know all the circumstances attendant on this matter. Furthermore, you have told me that Arabella does not choose her friends lightly, and consequently I would imagine that she could not be so fond of Serena were there not something to admire about her."

"Well," Lady Olivia said testily, "since you are determined to be the devil's advocate, I presume there is nothing more I can say."

He laughed. "You do make me very curious about this particular devil, my dearest Olivia."

Lady Olivia sighed and did not respond for certainly she had not meant to arouse her brother's always lively sense of curiosity. She should have remembered, she told herself crossly, that Adrian had a perverse streak that often drove him to take the unpopular side in any argument or cause and stubbornly stick to it; on occasion, he would wind up winning the argument and furthering the cause.

She wished that she had not spoken out so strongly against Serena and was even more regretful on that count when, a few hours later, Arabella said excitedly, "Papa is eager to leave for Brighton as soon as possible, Aunt."

"I am sure he is," Lady Olivia said tartly.

Arabella laughed and kissed her aunt, saying, "Let me thank you for all your fulminations against Serena. Obviously they have happily weighed in her favor."

"You and your father were born contrary, and I, for one, sincerely hope that you do not live to rue the day."

"I do not see how that could be possible. The lost is found; the prodigal son or, rather, daughter is returned; and I, for one, am delighted to provide the fatted calf," Arabella said ecstatically.

"And I hope that it will not turn out to be crow instead of calf," Lady Olivia snapped.

Unfortunately, Arabella did not hear her. She was already hurrying up the stairs and calling for Lizzie, her abigail, to instruct her to begin packing.

2

The eternal sound of the breakers advancing and retreating upon the brown pebbles of Brighton beach was in Arabella's ears, and in her eyes was a felicitous stretch of glistening wave-capped water, a sight she would see every time she gazed from her bedchamber. The magic through which her father had procured a sea-fronted suite on relatively short notice was something she had not understood until she had seen him speaking with the proprietor of their hotel, the Ship Hotel. That worthy had looked upon Lord Ashmore with actual affection, which, her father had subsequently explained, lay in a tip on a horse given years before and resulting in a sum that had refurbished a whole floor of chambers.

As Arabella turned away from the window, she dismissed that new knowledge along with Lord Ashmore's descriptions of the Prince Regent's and Mrs. Fitzgerald's Brighton sojourn as well as the transformation of the Marine Pavillion, which she would soon be visiting. None of these was as exciting as the thought of her pending reunion with Serena . . . Serena, about whom she had wondered, and over whom she had fretted, to the point that her teachers at school had warned that her distress was having a deleterious effect on her studies. They had insisted she make friends with the other girls, and at long length she had made the effort.

She had been more than rewarded for that effort, rewarded in two ways. She had made a friend of Camilla Deering, who lived in Hove, a town that lay just beyond Brighton, and Camilla had not only made up in part for the loss of Serena, she had noted the posters outside Brighton's Theatre Royal and had excitedly written to her telling her of Serena's presence in the town. Arabella intended to see Camilla, too, since she could easily make the short trip to the Ship Hotel. The three of them would have a most delightful reunion, she thought happily.

She glanced at the clock. It was close on four in the afternoon. They had taken the eight-hour journey to Brighton in easy stages, much to her secret regret. If she had had her way, they would have stopped only for meals. Unfortunately, Lady Olivia insisted on seeing some of the sights on the way. They had made side trips to ancient inns and churches and, at length, they had stayed overnight at Handcross. Arabella frowned, suspecting Lady Olivia of deliberately wasting time in order to postpone the moment when she should see Serena again. However, she quickly told herself that she was mistaken. That would have been devious and her aunt did not have a devious nature. She smiled wryly. Lady Olivia had once suggested that Serena had such a streak in her nature. For the thousandth time, she wondered why her aunt did not like her . . . But that did not matter, not anymore: she would soon be seeing Serena again. An anxious query directed to one of the hotel clerks had elicited the exciting information that the company, having been very well received, would be performing for another fortnight and might even be held over longer!

"Oh!" She clasped her hands as she gazed at the clock. "Will this evening never arrive?"

"Oh, would that this evening were over and done with," Serena said nervously to Mr. Julian Sherlay, the young actor who would be playing Sir Charles Surface in this evening's performance at the Theatre Royal. She added, "And I do wish all the people on this boardwalk would not stare at us as if we were wild animals in a menagerie! I do loathe it so."

Mr. Sherlay cocked a warm brown eye at his companion and said reasonably, "You might hate it even more if they did not, my dear Serena. And," he continued in his soft cultured tones, "it goes with our profession. Actors are always so regarded on and off the stage."

"I find it all very unpleasant," she complained.

"You must learn to take it with a grain of salt, my dear, and I do wish you would try to develop a sense of humor."

He received an uncomprehending stare. "About what, pray?"

"Life, my love." He laughed. His laughter ceased as he met another blank look. For a brief moment he was cast down. As usual, he quickly put a surge of disappointment behind him. There was so much about Serena that pleased him that he was well aware he should not cavil at the small deficiencies in her character—if, indeed, they could be called by so large a name. She knew nothing about irony or subtlety, and unfortunately, she had never learned to regard life as the great joke it actually was.

He smiled ruefully. Each time he thought of that, mentally he was back in the dingy purlieus of the

King's Bench Prison, put there by debts his father, counseled by Mark, his older brother, refused to pay. Mark, subsequently visiting him at the prison, had said with some satisfaction and pride that "we thought you must pay the price for your profligacy, Julian. It is time you learned your lesson."

It was to have been a lesson that would teach him respect, responsibility, and thrift—and that is where the irony had come in, but he had not to dwell on the King's Bench now. It was time to persuade Serena to run through her lines and to pray that she would speak them with some modicum of feeling. Maria was a small enough role, but it were better if it could be smaller yet. He was glad that Serena could not read his mind—glad on more than one count.

It was difficult to desire her and come up against that impregnable wall of respectability that she drew about her like curtains of iron. Yet, on occasion, just when he grew discouraged, she would give him languishing looks that set his heart to pounding and filled him with the hope that, in time, the gates would open. Of course, they would not open without a key, the key being a wedding ring, and he was trying to decide whether or not he should give it to her. Much as he loved her, he was not eager to settle down, not yet. He had spent nearly five months in the King's Bench Prison and it was an experience that had left him with a passion for freedom and a deep desire never to be behind those walls again. It also had left him with a need to enjoy his current lack of binding ties as long as he might. And besides, there was a little warning voice in his mind that counseled, "Wait."

He shrugged his thoughts away and said, "Here is

your cue, my love. 'Well, child, speak your sentiments.' ''

Serena clasped her hands, something he heartily wished she would not do. Then, in a manner he mentally and despairingly compared to that of a schoolgirl reciting a lesson learned by rote, she said, '' 'Sir I have little to say, but you shall rejoice to hear that he is happy; for whatever claim I had to his attention, I willingly resign to one who has a better title.' ''

"Serena, Serena," Julian protested in a tone edged with a sort of humorous irony. "Pray consider that poor Maria is hurt and angry at Charles, her lover, whom she believes unfaithful."

"I *felt* hurt and angry," she countered defensively.

"That is certainly a step in the proper direction," he said carefully, "but, my dear, you must communicate those feelings to me . . . you must also communicate them to the audience. It is not enough to stand there and look beautiful."

"Last night, there was a young man who said—"

"I heard what he said," he interrupted impatiently. "But he was not complimenting you upon your performance on stage, my love. He had quite another performance in mind, and that in his bedchamber."

Serena came to a dead stop. She gazed up at him indignantly, saying, "You should not s-speak to . . . to me in such abominable t-terms. You know that I . . . I would *never* . . . Oh . . ." She actually wrung her hands. "It is all so t-terrible to be thought a . . . a . . ."

"Whore?" Julian supplied.

She clapped her hands to her ears and turned an

indignant face up to him. "I will not listen, I tell you."

"Even though your own meaning was entirely clear?" he demanded, half-annoyed, half-amused at her self-delusion.

"I would never have said that . . . that *word*," she cried.

"No?" Julian laughed. "God pity us if the Gordons should decide to insert *'Tis Pity She's a Whore* into our schedule."

"Julian," Serena cried.

"Calm down, my love, it is a play by John Ford, and it is perfectly all right to call it by its true name without any of its onus leaking onto you. But enough, let us run through your speeches again, please."

"Julian, I know them and I must go on to the Ship Hotel, where I will meet with dearest Arabella—"

"No, Serena," he responded coolly, "you will not meet with 'dearest' Arabella. You will come back to the theater with me. It is close on six . . ." He gave her an accusing stare. "You did not tell me that you had a destination in mind—we are here to run over your lines."

Serena looked down quickly. "I did not actually have a destination in mind," she murmured. "I only thought—"

"You thought wrong," he interrupted edgily. "Now give me Maria's first speech, please."

Visiting a sulky, offended look upon his impervious countenance, Serena crossly obliged.

The Theatre Royal was filled to capacity, but by some magic he had not explained—but which Arabella thought might be due to the fact that her father held the title of earl—Lord Ashmore had acquired three seats in a box only one removed from the stage. Sitting at this vantage point, Arabella was able to see Serena very clearly, and in her excitement on first viewing her friend, she had quite forgotten her earlier disappointment in not receiving so much as a note from her at the hotel.

In fact, she had expected that Serena, in receipt of her joyous letter announcing their arrival, must have come to the hotel to greet her. However, she reminded herself that Serena probably needed to rest before her performance, and turned her attention on the play.

The curtain had fallen on the last act, and as the actors came forth to take their curtain calls, Arabella found herself in the throes of another disappointment: Serena's performance as Maria in a sprightly rendition of Sheridan's play, very well delineated by the rest of the cast.

Serena had looked beautiful, but she had uttered her few lines with no more animation than a waxwork. Indeed, Arabella had been unhappily reminded of those performances at school. Now, she avoided looking at her father and her aunt—particularly her aunt, who had muttered into her niece's ear, "She could never have won that role on acting ability alone, my dear."

A glance at her father showed her that he appeared amused. She winced. The other actors were fine, especially the young man who had played Sir Charles Surface. She smiled. Out of the corner of her eye, she had seen several other girls straighten in their seats and visit languishing glances on his handsome face each time he made an entrance. Now, as the actors stood bowing, she found herself dwelling on him rather than on Serena, and in that moment she realized that he was the man her friend had mentioned in her letter as being especially helpful to her. "Dear Julian," she had called him.

Judging from the way he was regarding Serena as they took their curtain calls, he had a strong reason for being helpful to her. He seemed much drawn to her friend. With an interior sigh, Arabella wished that he had been able to imbue Serena with some of his own acting ability. Then, with a surge of actual pain, she also wished that she were there instead of Serena.

She would have known how to interpret the role of Maria! She would not have stood there looking blank. Sir Charles would have received the full force of her indignation and Julian Sherlay would have had an actress to play against. A memory of how she had loved acting came rolling over Arabella like a breaker on Brighton's shores, drenching her with dissatisfaction. Alas, acting was not for her, daughter of a peer, and unless something untoward happened to prevent it—eventually wife to another peer.

She grimaced. Her father had solemnly promised that he would not force her into marriage, but she suspected Lady Olivia of pleading Lord Kinnard's cause. She winced. She would not dwell on that now. Her father had said that they would go backstage to see Serena, and with curtain calls finally at an end, she rose and, followed by Lord Ashmore and his sister, made her way down the stairs.

The crowds were dense. Quite a few people were heading in the same direction even though the play would be followed by a farce. It was only after turning to make a remark to her father that Arabella realized she had become separated from him and

Lady Olivia. It was futile to try to thread her way back to wherever they might be. She would have to go to the greenroom and hope they were there ahead of her or might join her presently. Unfortunately, she was not sure of its location. Glancing over her shoulder, she met the gaze of a tall, fair-haired young man.

"I . . . I beg your pardon, sir," Arabella said loudly enough, she hoped, to be heard in that laughing, chattering throng.

He bent an interested eye on her. "You are allowed to beg my pardon, my dear, but I cannot see that you have done anything to warrant that pardon."

Arabella laughed at this bit of nonsense. "I was wondering if someone could tell me how I might get to the greenroom, sir."

He smiled. "I would be more than delighted to show you the way." He moved to her side and put his arm around her waist. "Come, my dear."

"I do thank you, sir," she said gratefully, wondering if she ought not to protest his arm, but the crowds were dense and very probably he was afraid they might become separated.

"And why would you want to go to the greenroom, my dear?" her companion asked as he threaded his way through the throngs.

"I am meeting a friend."

"A friend . . . I see," he murmured. "A most fortunate friend, I am thinking."

Arabella was pleased to find the gentleman so knowledgeable. In a very short time he had escorted her into the greenroom, a chamber that appeared hardly large enough to accommodate a crowd that seemed to be composed mainly of gentlemen.

"Oh, I do thank you, sir," she said.

"I was most pleased to be of service," he replied genially. "Now, look your fill, my dear, and let us go."

"Go?" Arabella regarded him confusedly. "But I do not want to go. As I explained, I have come here to meet a friend."

His smile broadened and the pressure of his arm around her waist increased. "But, my lovely little ladybird, you have already found a friend, and I am he. Do not be afraid that I cannot meet the price of a prime article like yourself. I have more than enough of the ready. Now let us go."

Arabella tensed. She was not quite sure what he meant, but she did not like the look on his face and he was certainly speaking to her in far too familiar a way. "Sir," she said coldly. "As I have just explained, I am here to meet a friend." Determinedly, she tried to pull away from him, but his arm remained tight about her waist.

"My dear, I am quite willing to be your friend . . . and since you do not seem to have another 'friend' here, I suggest that we leave. Now."

"No," Arabella said loudly. "Let me go, sir. I have told you the truth."

"If you expect to increase your price, my girl," he began angrily, only to be confronted by a tall young man whom Arabella recognized as Julian Sherlay, the handsome actor who had performed the role of Sir Charles Surface.

"I do believe you are in error, sir," Mr. Sherlay said coldly. "This young lady obviously does not wish to go with you."

"Young . . . lady?" Arabella's captor laughed loudly. "She is a young lady, like you are a gentleman," he retorted. "This little doxy approached me and—"

"I asked you the way to the greenroom and you said you would show it to me," Arabella cried angrily.

"As nice an invitation to folly as I have ever heard, my pretty cyprian." Her captor grinned. "And believe me, I have heard many."

"It is not true," she cried.

"Of course it is not true," the actor snapped. "Anyone, even yourself, sir, can see that she is a lady, anyone who has not willfully donned blinders so that he might take advantage of an innocent." He stared fixedly at the other man. "Now get out," he ordered coldly.

Arabella's would-be seducer tensed. He glared at Julian. "You damned cur, daring to address your betters in so impudent a manner!" He advanced on Julian, his fists clenched. "You'll not be so appealing to the ladies when I have knocked your damned teeth down your swine's throat. And . . . Oof!" He went reeling back as Julian struck a heavy blow to his chin. "Damn you," he yelled in a greenroom grown suddenly very silent. "Keep your whore, then. I do not spill my claret fighting over doxies." He elbowed his way to the door and was out in minutes.

Arabella looked up at Mr. Sherlay. "I do thank you, sir. I am here to s-see Serena Spencer. We were at . . . at school together."

As her explanation dropped into the silence that had followed Julian's assault on Arabella's would-be seducer, there was a sudden burst of laughter, followed by resumed conversations heavy with comments on the scene that had just galvanized everyone in the chamber. Several young men—exquisites by the look of them—came up to pound Julian on the back and congratulate him. He smiled at them, but kept his attention on Arabella, raising his voice to say, "You are here to—"

"Arabella!" Lord Ashmore strode into the greenroom. "What are you doing here, and alone, pray?"

"Oh, father," she began unhappily. "We were separated by the crowds and this gentleman saved me from—"

"Arabella, my dearest!" Serena came to her side, looking confusedly from Julian to Lord Ashmore.

"Serena, oh, my dearest Serena." Arabella, seemingly oblivous of everyone save her long-lost friend, flung her arms around her. "Oh, I am so very happy to see you again."

"And I you, my dearest Arabella." Serena, equally effusive, kissed Arabella, her eyes widening as she looked at her. "But I would hardly have known you, you are grown so very beautiful!"

"Silly," Arabella said on a half-sob as she vainly tried to quell emotions that were threatening to get the best of her. "I have not changed a particle, but you . . . you are so lovely."

"My dear"—Lord Ashmore moved to Arabella's side—"will you not present me?"

"Oh, yes, Papa, of course." Arabella moved back from Serena saying hastily. "This is Serena Spencer, and this is my father, Lord Ashmore, and Papa," she added, "this is Mr. Sherlay, who struck down that horrid person, who seemed to think . . ." Tears suddenly blurred her vision. "Oh, it was all so terrible until he came."

Lord Ashmore stared at her concernedly. "Am I to understand you were accosted by someone?"

Arabella nodded. "But Mr. Sherlay intervened."

Lord Ashmore put an arm around his daughter's shoulders. "Poor child, it must have been a shocking experience." He smiled at Julian. "We are much in your debt, young man."

"It was nothing, my lord," Julian assured him hastily.

"I am inclined to believe the contrary—"

"You may do so, Papa," Arabella cut in quickly. "Mr. Sherlay gave that creature, who was trying to force me to go with him, a facer, is it not so called, Mr. Sherlay?"

"A facer, it is, milady," Julian corroborated with a smile.

"And where did you learn such a term, my dear?" Lord Ashmore demanded.

"It was when Timothy, who was taking me back from school, halted because of a street brawl. He was ever so interested. He said that one of the men had delivered a facer to the other," Arabella explained, blushing as her father and Mr. Sherlay laughed.

"And we wonder where comes the thieves cant on the tongues of certain, er, angels of the *ton*?" Lord Ashmore murmured.

"By such ways and such means, my lord." Julian grinned.

"I do believe, Adrian, that we ought to be returning to the hotel," Lady Olivia murmured, speaking for the first time and startling Arabella. She was subsequently embarrassed for not having introduced her aunt to Mr. Sherlay.

She was about to rectify that error when her father said, "Yes, we should return to the hotel and I would like to invite you both for a light supper. I hope that you, Miss Spencer, and you Mr. Sherlay will be my guests.''

"Oh, please,'' Arabella said quickly. "We would be delighted were you to join us.'' She scrupulously avoided looking at her aunt.

A quick glance passed between Serena and Julian and then she said, "We would be delighted, my lord.''

Lord Ashmore's green eyes reflected his smile. "The delight, Miss Spencer, is entirely mine.''

"Oh, it is so odd to hear you addressed as Spencer, Serena,'' Arabella cried. "Especially since I have known you so long as—''

"Oh, but you must call me Spencer,'' Serena broke in. "It is my stage name and I have become entirely accustomed to it.''

Something in her friend's manner told Arabella that Serena did not want her real name revealed. She said hastily, "Well, I do like it. It reminds me of Edmund Spenser, who wrote *The Faerie Queene*.''

"A most apt comparison, my dear,'' Lord Ashmore commented, his eyes on Serena's face.

Serena looked down, her lengthy dark lashes briefly covering her eyes as she said, "You are most kind, my lord.''

Arabella, watching this exchange, was delighted. She had hoped that her father would approve of Serena to the point that he would not decry her profession, and despite her aunt's disparaging remarks, it would appear that he had. She glanced at Julian Sherlay but failed to catch his eye, it also being bent on Serena.

A tiny tendril of regret stirred in her mind, Mr. Sherlay was staring at her friend in a most revealing manner. Obviously, he was in love with her, and why would he not be? Given their calling, he must be much in her society and without the encumbrance of a chaperon. To know Serena was to love her, and yet Arabella could not help wishing . . . She grimaced. Those wishes currently circulating through her mind and stirring her pulses were as futile as wishing on the moon. She glanced up at that heavenly body, seen through a small window in the greenroom. It was barely on the wane . . . Plenty of people believed that moon wishes were granted, but not this time, she was unhappily sure. She would not want to capture the attention of the young man who was regarding her friend so warmly. She could and would ask Serena about him, for, naturally, they would meet on the morrow.

"Well, let us go, then," Lord Ashmore said. "It is uncommonly stuffy in here."

"It is indeed," Julian agreed.

"We will show you a quick way out." Serena smiled up at Lord Ashmore.

"Please." He smiled back.

With Julian in the lead, they walked through a small passageway and in a very short time were standing on the boardwalk in front of the theater.

"Ah!" Lord Ashmore grinned. "There are ways and ways, I see." He looked down at Serena, his eyes on her moon-bathed countenance. "And so you were in school with my daughter," he murmured. "Yes, my lord, but I was forced to leave," she explained. "It was due to some of my father's unfortunate investments—funds, you know. It killed poor Papa."

"That is most unfortunate," he said concernedly. "I understand from my daughter that life was not too easy for you at first, and, indeed, I cannot imagine that it is easy now?"

"Oh, it is, my lord," she assured him. "I find the work much more pleasant, certainly. It was not easy being a governess and dealing with young children and their parents."

He gave her a long look. "I can imagine that the parents might, in some circumstances, be every bit as troublesome as the children."

Serena hesitated. Then she said slowly, "They can be difficult, my lord, the children, too."

"I am aware of that. I remember myself in early youth. My governess was a most miserable female."

Serena looked up at him. "I am inclined to believe that an entire exaggeration, my lord."

"It is," Arabella, who had been listening happy to this exchange, assured her. "He is on the best of terms with Mrs. Grinstead and still receives knitted mufflers from her at Christmas, as he did when he was a small boy."

"My love," her father reproved, "you are blackening my reputation."

Something in his tone caused Arabella to fear that he was rather displeased with her, but then he laughed and added, "Come, Olivia, my dear, do not fall behind, and you"—he turned to Arabella—"walk with me, please."

"Oh, may I not be with Serena?" she asked.

Serena said hastily, "I think I had best stay with Julian, but we can all five walk together."

"No, I think I will walk with Papa, then. I am sure that you and Mr. Sherlay wish to be together."

"You are right, to be sure, Lady Arabella." Julian smiled at her as he slipped an arm around Serena's waist.

She pulled back slightly. "Would not . . ." she began.

"Would not what, my darling?" Julian smiled down at her.

Raising her eyes to his moon-silvered countenance, Serena said softly, "Oh, dear, I have quite forgotten what I meant to say."

"Then, surely, it could not have been of great import," he said teasingly.

"No," she spoke hesitantly. "I do not believe it was."

Arabella, arm in arm with her father and with her aunt on his other side, said, "Oh, I am so happy."

"Are you, my dear?" Lord Ashmore asked. "I am glad of that. It was an excellent idea to come to Brighton."

"I am so pleased that you agree. And"—she lowered her voice—"I am glad that you like Serena. I did want you to like her."

"I am pleased to gratify your hopes." He nodded. "She reminds me of someone I knew in India."

"One of your dusky houris?" Lady Olivia murmured.

Arabella felt her father's arm tense. He said, "And what might you be meaning by that? There are white women in India, too, you know, Olivia."

"India . . ." Serena murmured. "You have lived in India. It has always been one of my dreams to visit it."

"Oh? And when did you dream that dream, my love?" Julian inquired with a laugh.

"I cannot remember when it first came to me," she said thoughtfully, "but it has always fascinated me. Such a strange mysterious place."

"And full of strange mysterious insects," Lady Olivia said crisply, "not to mention snakes on the ground, the trees, and in the streams. India is full of creatures with jaws, small and large, and with a regrettable tendency to exercise them on European flesh."

"Oh, Aunt Olivia, for shame," Arabella protested. "You have just robbed poor India of all its romance!"

"I certainly hope so," her aunt replied enigmatically.

"Ah, we have arrived at the hotel," Lord Ashmore proclaimed with a note of relief in his tones. "Come, we will toast the play and its players!"

"Oh, Serena!" Arabella had finally come face to face with her friend. "We will meet where, tomorrow?"

"Tomorrow?" Serena repeated confusedly.

"You said earlier that you wished to meet me after the rehearsal," Arabella reminded her with a touch of disappointment. "Did you forget?"

"Oh, no, well . . . yes, but you see, I have so very much on my mind," Serena murmured apologetically. "Come to the green room, my dearest. I am really eager to have a long talk with you."

"Oh, I will," Arabella assured her. "What time would you like me to come?"

"At two . . . yes, two in the afternoon. There is a chance I might be late, but please do wait for me."

"Oh, I will. I am not unused to waiting for you, Serena." Arabella laughed, visited by memories of all the times Serena had been late when they had made similar plans at school.

"So you are!" Serena giggled. "We will have a real talk and we will catch up on everything. It will be just as it used to be."

"Yes." Arabella gave her a loving look. "It will be just the same."

3

"And so, you have met the famous Miss Serena Spencer—or Sadlier, as we once knew her, Adrian," Lady Olivia said caustically once the actors had left. "And what did you think of her?"

Lord Ashmore met his sister's challenging glare with a smile. "I found her entirely charming, Olivia."

Arabella, who had bridled at her aunt's disparaging tone, threw her arms around her father. "I knew you must like her," she said warmly. "And, Aunt Olivia, I do not understand why you will hold to your dislike after all these years."

"All these years number no more than two, and I find her as I have always found her: far too conscious of an appearance that, I might say, my dearest, is no more felicitous than your own—to which I am sure your father must agree."

Lord Ashmore said, "They are different in type, certainly. Arabella is an English beauty, but Serena reminds me of certain females I knew in India. There is a touch of the exotic about her, I think."

"*And* the common," Lady Olivia sniffed.

"Well, well, here are certainly a pair of opposing points of view," her brother commented. "You do arouse my curiosity concerning this maiden."

"Maiden?" Lady Olivia echoed. "*I* would imagine

that she has left that state far behind, and unless I am deeply mistaken, she and that young man are lovers."

"You do not know that," Arabella cried.

"No, you do not, Olivia," Lord Ashmore agreed stiffly.

"Do I not?" She gave him a challenging stare. "They are *actors*, and actors are a law unto themselves—and I, for one, do not covet their society. I am going to bed, now." She glanced at Arabella. "It is certainly time that you retired, my dear Arabella, especially after the day you have had."

"Oh, I shall be coming to bed shortly, Aunt Olivia," Arabella assured her. She waited until the latter had left the room to say beseechingly, "You do not mind my friendship with Serena, do you, Papa? She was not always an actress."

He smiled at her. "No, my dear, I do not mind, and if you will pardon me for saying so, I do not really believe her an actress now."

Arabella burst into laughter. "She is not and never was. It is only her poverty and her horrid experiences as a governess that drove her into the profession. Poor Serena, she ought to be married. Perhaps Mr. Sherlay will offer for her."

"Do they have an understanding, then?" Lord Ashmore asked quickly.

"I do not know, though he seems very much in love with her, did you not believe so?"

Lord Ashmore said, "I fear I did not notice. It is late, my child. I suggest that we follow your aunt's excellent example and go to bed."

"Yes, I am a bit tired." Arabella nodded.

"And you ought to be, both emotionally and physically." He frowned. "You had a most unfortunate experience this night. You must never again go anywhere unescorted, my dear. That young man will not always be on hand to rescue you."

"No, I should not think he would be, Papa," Arabella said with the ghost of a sigh as she envisioned Julian Sherlay's handsome face and also the ardent looks he had visited upon the face of her friend. She did not want to envy Serena, she would not—or at least, she would make every effort not to do so, out of the very real love she bore this most favorite of all her friends.

On the day following her reunion with Serena, Arabella spent most of the morning trying to think of a way to elude her father and, also, her aunt's watchful gaze. Much to her surprise, one obstacle was removed when Lord Ashmore mentioned an appointment with a friend met by accident on the boardwalk while he was out for an early-morning stroll. He told Arabella that he would be gone for the better part of the afternoon.

Lady Olivia, meanwhile, had been in communication with an old friend, who had told her she would meet her in Brighton and had begged that she drop her a note on her arrival. Having punctiliously done so, she would be meeting her friend at the local lending library. Naturally, she had expected Arabella to accompany her and had looked displeased at her refusal. However, she agreed that the rest Arabella assured her she needed was a very sensible way for her niece to spend the afternoon.

"Undoubtedly, you are still feeling the effects of your unfortunate experience at the theater. To my way of thinking, you ought to have retired early, rather than encouraging your father to invite those actors to our hotel. I cannot understand Adrian, he never used to have a penchant for such low company."

"I cannot understand you, Aunt Olivia. Neither Serena nor Mr. Sherlay could be considered low company," Arabella had dared to retort. "They are both exceedingly presentable and well-spoken. And they are both obviously well-bred, too."

"If either had any pretension to good breeding, my dear, they would not be actors. It is all pretense with them."

"It is not pretense with Serena," Arabella exclaimed hotly.

"I cannot understand what you see in that girl."

"She is my best friend."

"A best friend who failed to communicate with you for nearly a year and a half?"

"I can understand that," Arabella retorted defensively.

Lady Olivia was silent a moment. Then, she said slowly, "The pity of it all is that *you* do not understand Miss—whatever she is calling herself now. You judge everyone by yourself. To my notion, it is most unfortunate that you have met up with her again. I can only hope that the company will soon move on."

While several answers to her aunt's observation rose to Arabella's tongue, none found its way to her lips. She was too pleased at her success in pulling a large hank of wool over her aunt's sharp eyes. She would meet Serena and think about possible consequences later. It occurred to her that she ought to take her abigail with her, but what would Lizzie do, cooling her heels while she and Serena caught up with the multitudinous happenings of the last year and three months? Besides, were she to go to the theater alone, she might catch a glimpse of Julian Sherlay and, better yet, exchange a word or two with him. She made a little face. During the previous night, she had dreamed of the handsome young actor, and at the thought of seeing him again, her face flamed.

Putting her hands up against her burning cheeks, she groaned and shook her head. It were folly to dwell on him. She must, must, must put him out of her mind! He loved Serena—that was obvious—and Serena loved him. That was equally obvious. And even if so formidable a barrier had not existed, there was an even more formidable barrier—or, rather a chasm—and that was, of course, his humble birth. Even were her father to sanction such a marriage, Julian would be unhappy since he could never be accepted by the *ton*. She laughed mirthlessly. She need not worry about that since Mr. Julian Sherlay was no more interested in her than he was in a fly on the wall! True, if they were to know each other better, he might like her, but he would never love her, not when his heart was entirely given to Serena!

On the pretext of a sick headache, Arabella dismissed a pleased Lizzie and generously gave her the remainder of the afternoon to do with as she pleased. Subsequently, she retired to her bed. Then, hurrying to the window, she was pleased to see Lizzie strolling down the boardwalk with Mark, the alternate coachman. Breathing a long sigh of relief, she rose and hurriedly dressed in a pale-yellow muslin walking ensemble. Slipping a book into her reticule in case Serena might be late for their appointment, a circumstance not entirely unexpected, she picked up her sunshade, also yellow, and hurried downstairs. Looking neither to the right nor to the left, she hurried across the lobby, and emerging from the hotel, she breathed a sigh of relief. She had been half fearful that some gentleman might accost her—but none had. Emerging from the hotel and ascertaining her direction, she set off for the stage entrance of the theater, where she had agreed to meet Serena. Fortunately, it was not far from the hotel.

"There will be a place inside where you will be able to sit down," Serena had explained. "And do not let old Toby, who stands like Cerebus at the stage door, intimidate you. Merely explain to him that you are waiting for me."

Serena's instructions brought her to the door, but though old Toby was crusty enough, he appeared less intimidating than concerned.

" 'Aven't seen 'er all this day, but may'ap she's still at 'er lodgings. You can go in and sit down, to be sure. 'Tis the first door on yer left along that passage. I 'opes she won't be keepin' you waitin' long . . . an', miss, should you see any young sparks come in there, pay 'em no mind, for 'tis sure they'll gi' you the eye."

"Oh, I shall not, and I do thank you," Arabella said.

She came into the greenroom, which looked very dim and unprepossessing by day, she thought. Without the glow from the chandelier, the walls were a muddy green and dust lay thick on the pictures and on the floor. Still, she liked the atmosphere, for beyond the greenroom lay the stage and a clock on the far wall must have alerted generations of actors that it was time to make their entrance. Also Mrs. Siddons might have occupied the same chair into which she was now settling down.

"If only . . ." she murmured, and hastily dismissed

the thought as she opened her reticule and took out her book, a work entitled, *The Gypsy's Curse*. It had been written by an author who did not want his name revealed but preferred to be called "The Unknown One." Actually, Arabella decided as she found her place, the work had probably been written by a woman. She could not imagine a man penning its breathless descriptions of one Myra Maltravers, deep in the dungeons of a shattered castle and seeing "something horrid in the shadows."

"Ah, beauty with a book," someone commented.

Arabella looked up quickly to see a tall, rakish young man in shabby but definitely stylish attire, smiling warmly at her. He continued, "I thought you must be beautiful, and you are."

"You are kind to say so, sir," Arabella said.

"I am less kind than honest," he observed. "Might one hope that you are the girl who is to read for Mr. Gordon this afternoon. You were to be here earlier—if you are."

"Alas, sir, I am not, but I do wish I were," Arabella sighed.

"And so do I," he agreed with an exaggerated sigh of his own.

"Are you taking on another member of the company, sir?" Arabella asked interestedly.

He shook his head. "Probably not, but Mr. Gordon does hear them if they ask to have an audition. We have some in every town who believe that they wish to be on the stage."

"Oh, do you?"

"Yes." He grimaced. "In every town and I read with 'em."

"Are many chosen?" she asked interestedly.

"Not many, no." He rolled his eyes. "And before

you ask me why, I will tell you that I would as soon hire a trained ape as some of those who have asked to be heard.''

"Oh, dear!" Arabella winced.

"Precisely," the actor said. "But if you are not here to read for us, might one ask why you are sitting in this far-from-pleasant chamber?"

"Actually, I am waiting for Miss Spencer," she explained.

"Alas, you will have a long wait, I fear. I saw the delectable Miss Spencer driving off with a most distinguished gentleman. I did not have the impression that she would return very soon, not the way he was looking at her and she, I might mention, at him. And . . ." He paused as the door to the stage opened and, much to Arabella's secret pleasure, Julian Sherlay emerged.

"Oh, Mr. Sherlay," she cried, inadvertently revealing that same pleasure as she cried, "I have been hoping I would see you."

He regarded her in amazement. "My dear girl, what are you doing here, and alone?"

"She is here to see our Serena," the other actor explained. "I was just telling her that the lady is not present, and judging from the handsome gentleman who bore her off in his coach, I would say that you are not without rivals, Julian."

Julian shrugged. "I have never been without rivals, Roderick, as I think you know."

"Ouch, hoist by me own petard!" The young man laughed. "It is not bad enough to be stabbed through the heart by Tybalt without you giving me a second slash?" He moved to Julian's side and patted him on the shoulder. "I do not think our hopeful actress will be arriving, and so I will leave you. Since I am dead for the rest of the afternoon, I will stroll up the boardwalk and let the sea breezes fan my visage. May I bid you good afternoon?'' He grinned at Arabella.

"You may, sir.'' She nodded. "Good afternoon.''

"Ah, would that I were a glove . . .'' he began soulfully and paused, "but I am out of my text. Alas, Mercutio is all swordplay and must leave the dalliance to others. Hail and farewell.'' Bowing, the actor left the room.

"He is charming.'' Arabella laughed.

"And quite mad.'' Julian grinned. "However, he is an excellent Mercutio and I may tell you that I am glad it was he whom you met here and no other.''

"I do not understand you, sir,'' she said confusedly. "I came here to meet Serena.''

"I am aware of that.'' He gave her a grave look. "And no, I fear you do not understand me. Might I know why you are here without your abigail, Lady Arabella?''

"I decided not to bring Lizzie with me. I thought I would be with Serena, you see.''

"That was very foolish.'' Julian frowned. "In leaving Lizzie behind, you are inviting advances from undesirable people. Mr. Traherne, fortunately, is not of their ilk, but surely after your unfortunate experience of last night . . .''

"As I told you, I was sure I would meet Serena,'' Arabella said with a touch of annoyance. "But it seems that she will not be here. I expect she forgot to send me a note.''

"She can be forgetful,'' he commented, a frown between his eyes. "And if young Mr. Traherne is not exaggerating, as he often does—''

"Oh, I am sure he must be,'' Arabella interrupted.

"She probably went out with some elderly relative—an uncle, no doubt."

"An uncle, no doubt." Julian nodded.

Looking at him, Arabella hoped that Serena had gone out with an elderly relative. She did not like to see him hurt and she had a feeling that he had been. She said, "I think I had best leave now."

"No," he said hastily. "You must not leave, not while there is no one to escort you back to your hotel. I came out for a moment only . . ." He hesitated. "Should you mind coming inside with me now? We are going to do the nightingale-and-lark scene and then I will be banish'd." He smiled at her. "We have rehearsed the end of the play earlier in order to accommodate Roger Clements, who is playing Friar Laurence and who had a pressing appointment."

"You actually mean that I might watch part of the rehearsal?" Arabella asked eagerly.

"Yes, if you do not mind."

"Oh, no, I do not mind. I should like it above all things!" She lifted glowing eyes to his face.

He looked pleased. "Very well, then. But I expect I need not tell you that you must be quiet."

"No, you need not tell me that, Mr. Sherlay," Arabella said solemnly. "I will not utter a word."

Coming into the theater, Arabella looked about her ecstatically enchanted by the sight of the half-lighted house and at the actors clad in everyday clothes, standing on a bare stage with chairs for props and chalk on the floor to mark entrances. They had not yet begun the scene and so she could say, albeit very softly, "Oh, Mr. Sherlay, it is lovely to be in a theater."

Julian regarded her with some surprise. "It is a

rather dreary place without its candles and its footlights."

"Oh, but it is not. I much prefer it this way. I have never been to a rehearsal—I mean, a real rehearsal."

He indicated a seat. "Well, this one will be brief. Stay there and wait for me."

"I will not stir," she said happily.

He walked up four steps onto the stage to be greeted by a rather querulous Mrs. Gordon. However, she quickly calmed down as in low tones that Arabella could not hear he evidently described his encounter with his fellow thespian and the reason for her presence there. Then, the rehearsal began and Arabella was amazed to see a mature Mrs. Gordon magically transformed into the youthful, ecstatic yet sorrowful Juliet—as she declared that it was the nightingale and not the lark . . . As for Julian, he was splendid as he delineated Romeo's youthful and ardent passion and his subsequent sorrow at leaving his love.

The scene ended and Julian was back with her once again.

"Oh, Mr. Sherlay," she breathed. "I have been in paradise."

"Paradise, is it?" he said amusedly as they went up the aisle and back into the greenroom.

"Oh, indeed it was," Arabella affirmed while they emerged from the theater and came blinking into the brightness of the street. "And soon must come the potion scene," she continued. Almost without volition, she said, " 'I have a faint cold fear thrills through my veins that almost freezes up the heat of life. . . . I'll call them back to comfort me. Nurse! What should she do here? My dismal scene I needs must act alone . . . come, vial!' " She lifted her cupped hands to her mouth and then took it slowly down. " 'What if this mixture do not work at all . . . shall I then be married tomorrow morning? No, this shall forbid it . . .' " She laid a phantom dagger down. " 'Lie thou . . . there . . .' " Hearing a noise in the street, Arabella paused and, looking quickly up at Mr. Sherlay, found him staring at her wide-eyed. She blushed, saying breathlessly, "I know the play very well."

"I can see that you do. I could also see the dagger as you laid it down and the potion in your hand. You more than merely know this speech, Lady Arabella. You feel it very strongly."

"Oh, yes, I do," she agreed softly. "I love it, love it, love it. I would give anything were I in Serena's position and could be employed as an actress."

"And with good reason," he said warmly. "It seems to me that Serena once told me she knew a girl who was a real actress, even though she had never appeared upon the professional stage."

"And never would . . ." Arabella corroborated sadly. "I expect she must have been talking about me. We used to do little scenes at school as part of our study of elocution." She managed a smile. "I once played Petruchio to her Kate. In fact, that was the last scene we did together. On that same afternoon, she was forced to leave the academy."

He regarded her thoughtfully. "And how was Serena's Kate?"

Arabella paused and then she said slowly, "Serena ought not to be an actress. She really ought to get married."

A shade passed over his face. "Yes, that is true. But

come, we must be on our way. Your aunt will probably be worried."

"She's not at home, nor is Papa," she said, hoping he had not resented her implied criticism of Serena, but she was rather sure that he agreed with her and was even more sure that he saw himself as Serena's husband. Consequently, he would not resent her frank comments.

As they came in sight of the hotel, Arabella, lifting her face to the cool breeze blowing off the ocean, said, "Oh, I do love the smell of the sea, and the sound of it, too."

"Do you?" he asked interestedly. "I do, too. I was born no more than a few miles from the ocean. We could see it from some of our windows."

"Oh, how lovely," she said, wondering if he came from fisher folk, but immediately that thought crossed her mind, she discarded it as ridiculous. Julian Sherlay, with his slender figure, his graceful hands, and his sensitive handsome face, could never have seen the light of day in a lowly cottage. She was suddenly sure of that—sure that generations of aristocratic ancestors were listed on his family tree.

"It *was* lovely, growing up near the sea," he agreed. "Must you return to the hotel immediately?" he asked rather abruptly.

She gave him a laughing look. "I expect I should. I do not imagine that my aunt will remain in the lending library all afternoon, and I do not know where my father has gone—but as long as you see me almost to my door but do not come inside with me, I should love to remain on the boardwalk a little longer. It is only my second day in Brighton."

"Then, of course, you must remain on the

boardwalk a little longer, and I promise faithfully to vanish like a bottled genie ere I am sighted by the wrong eyes.''

"Oh, you are kind,'' Arabella said gratefully.

"Oh, I am not, unless it is a kindness to find oneself with a beautiful and talented young lady and be able to enjoy some part of a pleasant afternoon with her.''

To cover a sudden rush of happiness, Arabella said, "I do thank you for the compliment, sir.''

He came to a stop and said quite seriously, "But I am not complimenting you, Lady Arabella. I am speaking the truth—a rather sad truth, I fear.''

She regarded him with no little surprise. "A sad truth, sir?''

Almost fiercely, he said, "It is a pity to see such talent go to waste.''

"Oh, sir,'' Arabella murmured, smiling at him. "If you have enjoyed it, my talent has not gone to waste.''

He regarded her in surprise. "You are quite, quite unusual, Lady Arabella. I can now understand why Serena was so pleased when she received your letter . . . and at the same time, so very sorry that she had not communicated with you.''

"Is that really true?'' Arabella asked eagerly.

"It is entirely true,'' he assured her. "So I beg you will not take it to heart that she did not meet you this afternoon.''

"Oh, I do not,'' Arabella said as they started walking again. "I expect that something untoward detained her.''

"Precisely,'' he agreed, but there was a slight frown in his eyes. Then, looking up, he added, "But look at the sea gulls—they seem to be flying in a pattern.''

''Oh, they are,'' she agreed, gazing at them and enjoying a sudden breeze that was cooling her face and running through her hair like phantom fingers. She shifted her gaze to the foam-edged water and laughed as she watched a mule-drawn bathing machine bouncing over the pebbled beach. ''Oh, dear, I do loathe the idea of being dipped!''

''As I do myself,'' he agreed. ''It is a poor way to enjoy the sea. One ought to have the freedom of the waters.''

''The freedom, yes,'' she agreed, suddenly all too aware of the restraints upon her and resenting them. In fact, though she had never given much thought to those restraints, at this moment it seemed to her as if she were actually enslaved by them.

''What have I said, Lady Arabella?'' he inquired. ''Something untoward, I fear.''

She gave him a startled look. ''Why, nothing untoward,'' she assured him. ''What makes you imagine that you did?''

''You seem unhappy,'' he observed.

''But I am not! I could never be unhappy . . .'' She paused. She had been about to say ''with you,'' but hastily thought better of it, adding instead, ''On such a lovely day.''

''It *is* a lovely day,'' he agreed, regarding her quizzically. ''Yet, why do I have the feeling . . .'' He paused, frowning. ''Do you know, I think we must go back.''

She was surprised and confused by that sudden decision and also by the brusqueness with which he had phrased it. But she guessed that he had a reason for it. He had begun to worry about Serena and her inexplicable absence. Probably, she decided, it was not really inexplicable. At school, her friend was always going off by herself and returning without explanation or apology. She had often been scolded for it by her annoyed instructors. Then a little tendril of hurt slid into her mind. Considering their long separation, she wished that Serena had not been seized by one of those moods, moods she had forgotten until now and was glad, suddenly, that she had remembered them—since they did provide an explanation for her nonappearance at the theater. Mr. Traherne, she recalled, had also provided an explanation, but she did not believe him, no matter what Mr. Sherlay said about his truth-telling! She said, "Yes, I expect we must go back."

"Come, then." Mr. Sherlay nodded, quickly changing his direction.

As they came into the lobby, Arabella, having forgotten that she had not wanted him to come so far with her, caught sight of her aunt. She was standing near the desk and looking extremely anxious. Arabella started to ask him to leave quickly, but in that same moment Lady Olivia saw them. She came forward hastily, but much to Arabella's relief, she had a welcoming smile for her companion.

"Good afternoon, Mr. Sherlay," she said graciously. However, it was a graciousness that faded quickly as she turned to Arabella. "Where have you been?"

Since nothing but the truth could suffice, Arabella said reluctantly, "I went to meet Serena at the theater, but she was not there. Mr. Sherlay insisted on escorting me back."

"Oh, I am glad of that. I do thank you for

insisting, Mr. Sherlay," Lady Olivia said. Before he could respond, she added, "Arabella appears to believe that the streets of Brighton are as safe as those in our village—and meanwhile Lord Kinnard has arrived and has been asking for you."

"Lord Kinnard is here?" Arabella said with a grimace.

Her aunt's expression very nearly mirrored her own. "He is here and mightily put out that you were not on hand to greet him. And . . . Oh, dear," she broke off as Lord Kinnard, a stocky young man, dressed in the height of fashion, came across the lobby, his full face flushed. He reached them in a minute, and apparently oblivious to all save Arabella, he bowed over her reluctantly extended hand, saying, "Ah, at long last you have returned." Then, moving back, he looked blankly up at Julian, who was several inches taller than himself. His gaze lingered on the actor's neat but rather shabby attire, and then he looked rather confused.

"Have I not seen you somewhere before, sir?" Lord Kinnard demanded.

"If you were at the theater last night, you have, sir," Julian responded equably.

"Mr. Sherlay is playing the role of Sir Charles Surface in *School for Scandal*, which the company presented last night. I went to the theater this afternoon to meet a friend. She was not there and he was kind enough to bring me back to the hotel," Arabella explained, and under cover of her long lashes, she scanned Lord Kinnard's countenance for the shock she anticipated. She was not unrewarded.

Lord Kinnard looked as if he had suddenly inhaled a particularly offensive odor. He said coldly, "I take it that you are an actor, sir?"

"Yes, I am here in Brighton with the Gordon troupe," Julian explained.

Digesting this information, Lord Kinnard said with a hauteur that bordered on the offensive, "Well, my man, I am indeed grateful that you brought Lady Arabella back."

"It was my pleasure, my lord." Julian bowed while Arabella, gazing at Lord Kinnard's lowering countenance, was hard put not to giggle.

Lady Olivia said, "I, too, am grateful that Arabella met Mr. Sherlay at the theater." She shook her head. "You certainly ought not to have gone there alone, my dear."

"I am quite aware of that now," Arabella said. "I will not do so again."

"I should hope not," Lord Kinnard exclaimed. "But I expect we must needs allow for your innocence, my dear." He fastened a chill gaze on Julian's face. "It was fortunate you were present, my man. I would like to, er, reward you for—"

Arabella gasped and exchanged a lightning glance with her aunt, whose face mirrored her own shock, while Mr. Sherlay said icily, "Rewards are for porters, my lord. If you will excuse me, I will bid you good afternoon." Turning on his heel, he strode out of the hotel.

"Well," Lord Kinnard said, "the fellow seems mightily above himself, I must say."

Arabella glared at him. "How could you insult him in that horrid manner," she demanded angrily.

"I insult *him*?" Lord Kinnard regarded her in consternation. "My dear, you are truly an innocent. One does not insult persons of that ilk. Actors are forever out of pocket and generally they are not so stiff-necked." He smiled. "I expect it was your presence kept his hand in his pocket. He was looking at you in a most familiar way, Lady Arabella.''

"Come, my lord, you do refine upon it far too much,'' Lady Olivia said coolly. "I myself would not have offered him a reward.''

"But how else might I have thanked him for her safe return? You'd not have had me treat him to a meal, I hope?'' Lord Kinnard asked confusedly.

"You were not required to make a gesture of any kind,'' Arabella said, trying to keep a mounting rage from coloring her tones. "I thanked him for bringing me back to the hotel and so did Aunt Olivia. I am sure that was all he required.''

Lord Kinnard smiled contemptuously. "I am afraid, my dear Lady Arabella, that you are not as well-acquainted with the acting fraternity as I am. That fellow was deucedly slim, and I am sure that from time to time he is glad of the scraps from someone's kitchen table.'' Before either lady could respond, he continued, "Do I understand that you went to the theater to meet a friend, Lady Arabella?''

"Yes, you did. One of the actresses was my best friend at school. She suffered financial reverses and went into the theater.''

"I see,'' he said coldly. "You are, I expect, to be congratulated for your loyalty. Still, were I you—''

"But you are not, Lord Kinnard,'' Arabella said freezingly. "And Serena is still my very best friend.''

"And of a good family, too,'' Lady Olivia said, surprising her niece.

"Surely, she could have found a more felicitous sort of employment,'' he said with a frown.

"My friend is exceedingly beautiful, Lord Kinnard,'' Arabella said. "And she found to her sorrow that she received far too much interest from the gentlemen in the households where she was employed as governess. I am sure that you are not unfamiliar with such situations.''

"If a young woman minds her own business . . ." he began stiffly.

"I fear, my lord, that even then, she is not free from unseemly advances," Lady Olivia commented. "I was once a governess—at a time when our family had suffered reverses. And I can assure you that though I made every effort to be as inconspicuous as possible, there were still gentlemen who were only too eager to pursue me."

Lord Kinnard looked extremely annoyed, but he said, "I imagine, Lady Olivia, that since you are very well-looking now, you must have been quite lovely."

"Nonsense," she snapped. "I looked little different than I do now—a woman without resources is often pursued, my lord."

"No doubt," he said uncomfortably. "If you will excuse me, since I have only recently arrived, I must retire to my chamber. May I hope that I can await upon you tomorrow, Lady Arabella?"

She stifled a sigh. "I am not sure of my father's plans for the morrow, Lord Kinnard. It is probably best that you consult him."

"I will do that, of course, Lady Arabella. I will bid you good afternoon."

As she reluctantly stretched out her hand, saying, "Good afternoon, my lord," he carried it to his lips, and after pressing too long and too wet a kiss upon it, he bowed to her and to Lady Olivia and left them.

"Oh, dear," Arabella groaned, watching him stride toward the stairs. As soon as he started to mount them, she wiped her hand on her skirt, adding, "I did not expect to see him in Brighton. I wonder how he knew we were here?'' She turned an accusing stare on her aunt. "Or do I have to wonder?''

She received a regretful look from her aunt. "You do not. It is my fault, but I did not reveal that information on purpose. In making your excuses on a day when you insisted you'd not see him, I explained that we were soon to leave London for Brighton and that you were at the mantua maker's. Pray accept my apologies, child, I truly am sorry.''

Arabella still regarded her suspiciously. "Are you really, Aunt Olivia? For all you say that you do not like him—''

"I do not like him,'' her aunt interrupted. "I find him singularly similar to those gentlemen who were wont to pursue me in the garden when I was working as a governess. And I am of the opinion that he might be quite obnoxious if given the opportunity.''

"Oh, I do hope that Papa is of your opinion, Aunt Olivia.''

"I am reasonably sure that he is. In fact, I imagine that he will welcome his presence in Brighton no more than we. His lordship's only claim on your father rests on the fact that the late Lord Kinnard was Adrian's good friend in the days before he went to India.''

"Oh, dear, Papa never told me that,'' Arabella said apprehensively.

"I do not believe my brother will let his sentiment outweigh his judgment, my love, but let us go upstairs on the off chance that Lord Kinnard might take it into his mind to return to the lobby.''

"Yes, by all means, do let us hurry and seek the sanctuary of our suite.'' Arabella started for the stairs.

As they came into the small drawing room that lay

between their chambers, Arabella, gazing anxiously at her aunt said, "You are quite sure that Papa does not favor Lord Kinnard?"

Looking into her niece's concerned face, Lady Olivia said bracingly, "I am quite sure, my dear. You have had, unfortunately, scant opportunity to know your father as I know him. Still, I can assure you that since he married for love, I am positive that he will want you to do the same."

"That is comforting, Aunt Olivia," Arabella said, but on coming into her own chamber, she wondered what Lady Olivia and her father would think were they to become aware that she had already fallen hopelessly in love with one Julian Sherlay, actor. With a sigh, she told herself that it was useless to dwell on a passion that must remain forever unsatisfied, since the gentleman in question was hardly aware of her existence.

"But," she murmured, "even though it did not start out that way . . . it has proved to be a lovely day." With a feeling of great surprise, she remembered what she had been well on the way to forgetting. Serena had not kept their appointment. Why? She did not really want to know the reasons—she was only glad that she had not come.

4

"Oh, I did enjoy the *Romeo and Juliet*, Aunt Olivia. Did you not?" Arabella asked.

Her aunt smiled at her. "If I were to count the number of times you have asked me that since we saw it last night, you would be surprised. And I will say as I said before, yes, Mr. Sherlay is a notable Romeo. He turned in as good a portrayal of the role as I have ever seen, and Mrs. Gordon, though a trifle mature for Juliet, did very well. She quite made my blood run cold in the course of her potion scene."

"I thought so, too. And though she did not have a speaking role, I think that Serena was a lovely Rosalind."

"It was well she did not have a speaking role," Lady Olivia said dryly. "But I will agree that she did look lovely."

"Papa *likes* her," Arabella said pointedly. "He praised her grace in the dances. You will be pleasant to her when she comes this afternoon, will you not?"

"I have said that I will, if she arrives," Lady Olivia said pointedly.

"She will arrive," Arabella insisted. "She was most apologetic about not meeting me at the theater. You heard her. She said that she would explain everything today."

"Um . . . I suppose I need not emphasize the fact that you might have been in grave difficulties, staying alone in the greenroom for so long a time?"

"But I was not, Aunt. I had a most agreeable time as I have already explained."

"A stroke of luck your dearest friend could not have anticipated."

"But Serena would have known that Mr. Sherlay would be there, and the other actor was very kind to me, also."

"I still say . . ." Lady Olivia began.

"Oh, gracious," Arabella said crossly. "I should never have mentioned . . ." She paused at a knock on the door. "Oh, that will be Serena!" she cried excitedly. She was prevented from flying into the outer chamber to open the door by her aunt, who murmured, "Your abigail will admit her."

Shown by Lizzie into the large chamber that served both as dining and receiving room, Serena arrived looking very like she always had at school, her hair just a smidgen windblown and wearing a plain blue dimity gown. All vestiges of the poised actress appeared to have vanished as, seemingly unaware of Lady Olivia, she said warmly, "Dearest Arabella, at last!"

"Serena, my dearest." Arabella hastened to embrace her, feeling now as if they were greeting each other for the first time after their long separation. "Oh, I am so very happy to see you!" Belatedly remembering her manners, she added, "And here is Aunt Olivia."

"Lady Olivia." Serena dropped a curtsy and some of her warmth vanished as she continued, "I am so pleased to see you."

"And I, you, Miss Sadlier . . . Oh, dear, I do mean Spencer."

Serena smiled. "If you choose to call me Sadlier, I am amenable, Lady Olivia, though Spencer is the name I have chosen for my stage appearances."

"Well, since it is difficult for me to think of you except as Arabella's little friend from school, I think I will choose Sadlier." Lady Olivia's smile did not quite erase the sting of her words.

Arabella said quickly, "Unlike my aunt, I have mastered Spencer, but if you do not mind, I will continue to address you as Serena."

Serena's laugh was not quite genuine. "But, of course, you must always call me Serena, my dearest Arabella."

"I cannot imagine a time when I would not." Arabella indicated a sofa. "Let us sit down."

"And let me see to refreshments," Lady Olivia said. "I am sure you both have a very great deal to discuss."

"Yes, we have a very great deal," Arabella agreed, hoping that she did not appear too relieved, but if she did, her aunt had no one but herself to blame, with her unkind implication that she regarded Serena merely as a friend from school rather than an actress with a touring company. Yet, on second thought, given the onus attendant on acting, perhaps she was being merely polite. She waited until her aunt had left the room before saying, "Oh, Serena, dearest, now we can really talk!"

"Yes, finally," Serena smiled. "And the first thing I wish to say is that I am so very sorry that I did not join you at the theater. Julian scolded me roundly for letting you come to the greenroom alone. He said that you could easily have been accosted by someone undesirable."

"But I was not," Arabella assured her hastily. "In fact I had a most enjoyable time. Besides, I am sure that you had your reasons for not coming."

"I did." Serena rolled her eyes. "The most fortunate set of circumstances, my dear. You see, I have relatives in Hove and my cousin Bertram descended upon me just as I emerged from my lodgings and said that I must come to my Aunt Elvira's bedside because she was ill and calling for me."

"Oh, dear, I hope it was not a mortal illness."

"No," Serena said grimly. "But, as usual, she believed it was and had invited me there, if you can imagine, for the express purpose of telling me that she intended to settle her money on my cousin Bertram, her son, of course, and my cousin Celia, who is more distantly related to her than I, but who is not an actress. She implored me to repent of my horrid profession and renounce my evil ways and join the Methodists before I was doomed to ever-lasting flames. That, my dearest Arabella, was my day, and if you only knew how much rather I would have been with you . . . But of course, you must know."

Arabella laughed. "Oh, dear, alas for romance. Your cousin must have been that 'handsome gentle-man' who, Mr. Traherne said, picked you up."

"Damn and blast Mr. Traherne," Serena said roundly. She flushed as she met Arabella's surprised look. "I am sorry, my dear, but he does annoy me, with his nasty implications. Bertram is not in the least handsome, but leave it to Mr. Traherne to make something up out of whole cloth! And I understand that he made the most shocking advances to you."

"Fortunately, he was restrained by Mr. Sherlay. If your aunt is in Hove, does she know Camilla Deering? I had hoped to see Camilla, but I received a note from her saying that she was going to Cornwall to see her aunt and uncle. It was she who told me that you were here."

"Yes, I remember you telling me that." Serena smiled. "Do you know, Arabella, you are really so very kind. If I were you and I had been kept waiting at the theater, I should have been furious. Pray forgive me, but I was so exercised over the matter with my ghastly relatives that I even forgot to send you a note. And Julian scolded me roundly for that, I can tell you."

"I did not mind, for Mr. Sherlay invited me in to watch the rehearsal until he could escort me back to the hotel. Oh, Serena, he is a wonderful actor."

"Yes, he is quite accomplished," Serena allowed. "I expect he is the best in the company."

"Oh, yes, indeed, he is. And he is also such a pleasant person. We had a lovely walk."

"A walk?" Serena gave her a quizzical look. "Oh, from the theater. He told me he took you back to your hotel."

"We also strolled up the boardwalk for a bit . . . to see the dippers. He agrees that it is a poor way to go swimming."

"Oh, indeed?" Serena raised eyes that held a chill, disapproving expression in them. "I must say that I am surprised at Julian, taking you so far from the hotel and without a chaperon. I am also surprised that you would consent to go with him, considering the proprieties involved."

Arabella regarded her with an understandable

amazement. "We did not walk very far, nor were we out long. He said that I must return to the hotel. As for the proprieties involved, I am sure that no one was the wiser."

"You were fortunate," Serena said coolly. "I will have to speak to Julian, I see."

"Oh, pray do not," Arabella said.

"I think I must, my dear," Serena said stubbornly. "Obviously he does not have any notion how the daughter of an earl must be treated. As I have suggested, Julian, in common with most actors, is a nobody from nowhere."

Arabella regarded her with a mixture of distress, disappointment, and anger. She had never seen Serena in this mood before and it occurred to her that her ire might be prompted by jealousy—but how could she be jealous when Julian's every look, every gesture showed him to be deeply in love with her? She said with a touch of indignation, "That cannot be true, Serena. Mr. Sherlay is very much the gentleman. I would not be surprised if his birth were as gentle as our own."

Serena laughed. "An actor? You do not find members of the *ton* among the actors, I assure you. They are all pretense. They pretend on the stage and off the stage, except when they are together, trading crude jokes and making horridly lewd suggestions. They have no morals at all. You do not know actors as I do, my dear Arabella, and pray God you never will."

"You are not happy being in the theater, are you, Serena?"

"No, my dear," Serena said with a touch of sarcasm. "I am not happy being in the theater."

"I do not understand you. How could you not be

happy with Mr. Sherlay, who loves you so much?''

"Oh? He has confided in you, then?'' Serena raised her eyebrows.

"No, nor does he need to confide in me—when it is so entirely obvious.''

"Obvious? Is it?'' Serena looked momentarily pleased. Then, she sighed and shook her head, saying with a frown, "I expect he does care for me. Oh, dear, if only he were not an actor. They have no social standing—people do not respect them or, rather, us. If you knew the number of insults that have been leveled at me . . .''

"Oh, God, Serena, if I could be an actress, I would take every insult with a grain of salt and laugh in the faces of those who insulted me,'' Arabella cried passionately. "I love acting. I would love to be an actress.''

"No, you are not being truthful, Arabella.'' Serena rose and took a turn around the room, coming back to where Arabella sat and staring down at her. "You love the idea of acting. You love it in safety and in luxury. Look at this chamber, this suite, it is palatial compared to some of the holes where the members of our company are forced to reside. You have never known what it is to rise in the morning while it is still dark and go off to another town . . . And try to find lodgings and have the innkeeper look at you as if he expected you to put his silver in your reticule. You have no idea how often a constable will appear at the stage entrance and haul some actor off to jail because one or another member of the audience has leveled a complaint at him. They might not like the cut of his suit or the way their lady fair looked at him . . . and he languishes there until the company manager buys his release, which he cannot always afford to do.

Then, there are the local gentlemen who find an actress fair prey, as it were. One of our girls was kidnapped while we were playing in Bristol a few months ago.

"She was not brought back until the following afternoon. She was in hysterics and she had been with a young man who had hurt her cruelly. Mr. Gordon complained to the constable and was ordered out of town. I myself have often been approached. Fortunately, I am no frightened child. I have not hesitated to tell any would-be seducer what I thought of him. Some of them have been very angry, indeed, but they have left me alone. Still, I might not always be so fortunate, Arabella."

Listening to her, Arabella felt sorry for her, but she was also surprised, wishing that Serena could put such passion into her acting. Were that possible, she could be another Mrs. Siddons. She said carefully, "It does appear to be a hard life, but were you wed to Mr. Sherlay . . . You do seem to love him and . . ."

Serena frowned. "I have thought I loved him," she said slowly. "However, I cannot love the fact that he appears to be content with this life. Actors are not respectable. They can never be respectable, not even if they are a Garrick or a Kemble! They are actors, entertainers. Julian has told me that in the old days, actors wore collars like dogs."

"That was centuries ago!" Arabella exclaimed.

"All the same, I want something more. I deserve it. I come from a good family. My mother . . . but I am not telling you anything you do not know. I do not want to spend my life on the road!"

"Oh, my dear, you have everything, everything in the world to make you happy."

Serena gave her a long hard look. "You, my

dearest Arabella, have been allowed to remain a child, a romantic child. I, unfortunately, though no more than a year older than you, have been required to grow up. I have grown up in a world where romance is something one finds only in books and plays. There is precious little of it in life, my dear friend, my dear innocent friend.''

Arabella regarded her with a mixture of surprise and hurt. It seemed to her that Serena resented her so-called innocence as much as she mocked it. Furthermore, she must have misunderstood what she had been saying.

"I was not speaking about romance, Serena. I was speaking of being in the theater. Despite what you say about acting, I would give a great deal to be an actress, and it is not a childish ambition, as you seem to believe. Even Mr. Sherlay told me that I had talent.''

"Did he?'' Serena frowned. "How did he divine that?''

"I recited something from *Romeo and Juliet*—part of the potion scene.''

Serena gave her a condescending smile. "I am sure that he was being kind, my dear. Julian is very kind. It is one of the traits I love about him. Oh, dear, if only he were not an actor.''

Arabella swallowed an angry retort regarding Mr. Sherlay's so called "kindness.'' That had been unkind on the part of Serena, she thought, but immediately reminded herself that her friend was very unhappy and certainly she, who had no feeling for acting, could not appreciate her own passion. She said merely, "What would you prefer Mr. Sherlay to be?''

"A gentleman, I expect, a rich gentleman, but I

imagine that I sound very mercenary and . . ." Serena gave her a long, penetrating look. "I think I have hurt you, Arabella. I never meant to do that. Pray put it down to my dissatisfaction with my own lot in life. It is truly ironic—I, who have cherished propriety above all else am an actress, but I fear I have neither the enthusiasm nor the talent to be worthy of the name."

"Why ever did you find work in the theater, then?" Arabella could not help asking.

"It found me, my dear. My poor father had been a tutor and among his pupils had been Mr. Gordon. Shortly after I had been ignominiously dismissed from my last position as a governess because the young master had made advances to me and been slapped across the face for his pains, my father met up with Mr. Gordon and told him about my trouble. He asked to meet me, and the rest is what you see."

"Oh, poor Serena." Staring into her friend's disconsolate face, Arabella felt very sorry for her, realizing that the respectability Serena desired so deeply more often than not proved to be another chimera. But how tell her that, who felt herself among the dispossessed and the denigrated? She suddenly wished that there were some fairy who could wave a magic wand so that they might change places, and she could have her chance to act and Julian's love, while Serena would have the respectability and the high position she coveted.

At this point and much to her surprise, her father came in, stopping just beyond the door, his eyes widening, "Good afternoon, my dear Arabella, and Miss Spencer, how very pleasant to see you again."

Serena rose to drop a curtsy. "And you, my lord," she murmured.

"Pray take your seat, Miss Spencer," he begged. He turned to Arabella, "My dear, I met Lord Kinnard on my way here."

"Oh, dear, did you?" she sighed.

"He asked to see me on a most important matter," he smiled.

"Oh, would he want to offer for you, Arabella?" Serena breathed.

Arabella gave her friend a long-suffering look, then, turning to her father, she asked edgily, "Are you going to see him, Papa?"

"I did give him a time, my dear."

"How very exciting, Arabella!" Serena murmured.

Arabella visited a lackluster stare on Serena's face and turned to her father. "What do you intend to tell him, Papa?"

He smiled at her, "I imagine I shall tell him that my little chick is not quite ready to leave her nest and that I intend to enjoy her presence a little longer. Does that please you, my dear?"

"Oh, Papa," Arabella ran to him and gave him a quick hug, saying as she stepped back, "Thank you so very much! I do dislike him—*completely*."

He regarded her gravely, "Then we'll not consider him at all, my dear. I will leave you to chat." He turned to Serena. "I expect you will want to go to the theater, Miss Spencer. May I drive you there later?"

"Oh, my lord,"—she smiled up at him—"that would be most kind."

"And I will come with you!" Arabella exclaimed.

"My dear, I fear that would not be convenient," he said regretfully. "Directly I have taken Miss Spencer to the theater, I must leave for a dinner engagement."

"Oh, I see . . . Well, some other time, then," Arabella said.

"Yes, of course, any other time, my dear." He bowed to the two girls and strode out of the room, closing the door behind him.

"He is so charming, your father," Serena commented.

"Oh, I am pleased that you think so. He *is* charming, and it is lovely having him home again."

"It must be. I remember that you saw him very seldom while we were at school."

"Yes, actually I am just getting to know him, really. There were times, if you will remember, when he did not come home at all."

"But now he is back from India for good?" Serena pursued.

Arabella nodded, "He is anxious to turn his attention to the estates."

"It is a pity you did not see him more often while you were growing up," Serena said thoughtfully. "Still I imagine that there were some girls who would as lief not have seen their fathers at all. Do you remember Eva Kenmore, who said she lived in a castle in Scotland?" Serena giggled. "And it turned out to be a hostelry called the Castle Inn and her father was the innkeeper?"

"Oh, yes, I do, poor thing," Arabella said.

"She was *not* a poor thing," Serena said coldly. "She was a horrid snob and tried to queen it over the rest of us. She deserved to be unmasked. My, she was so crestfallen. And . . ." She paused as the abigail entered with a tray that she placed on the table near the sofa where the girls were conversing. On it were tea, cakes, and fruit.

"Oh, how delightful!" Serena exclaimed, as the

girl curtsied and went out. "But will your aunt not be joining us?"

"I expect she wishes to leave us alone, since we've not seen each other in such a long time," Arabella explained.

"And I also expect that she wants to see as little of me as possible," Serena commented. "She never has liked me."

"You mistake her manner," Arabella hastened to assure her. "She has always been withdrawn even with me."

"You were always adept at pouring oil on the troubled waters. Do you remember that time at school when Lizzie Carew was about to be expelled and . . ."

"Oh, I do, and do you remember . . ." Arabella began.

In the time that followed, the friends conversed about school and the theater, mainly because Serena appeared unwilling to describe her experiences upon leaving the academy. She was very eager to discuss some of the amusing episodes she had witnessed while with the Gordon Company such as the time Mr. Gordon, playing Othello, went outside the theater during a rainstorm and, being in danger of missing his cue, rushed on with streaks of white amid the black. A critic for a local paper had called him the "zebra Moor." And there had been the gallant who had tried to have his way with her right on stage and Julian had throw him into the pit. They had left town very quickly that night because, Serena explained, the gallant had been a noble and Julian, as a lowly actor, had risked jail.

"How he must love you!" Arabella commented.

"I expect he does," Serena shrugged.

"You are very cool about it, I must say," Arabella said indignantly.

"My dear," Serena began in a slightly patronizing

voice. "Actors . . ." She paused as Lord Ashmore entered, dressed for his evening appointment.

He was looking uncommonly handsome, his daughter thought, and amazingly youthful. In fact, he could have been at least five years younger than he actually was—not that thirty-nine was old. He had been a mere twenty-one when she was born and her poor mother seventeen, dying an hour after her birth —but now was no time to dwell on that.

"Papa," she said chidingly, "you've not come to take Serena away already?"

"Already?" he echoed. "My love, do you not realize that it has been close on three hours since last I looked in on you?"

"Indeed?" Arabella breathed. "You must be funning me."

"I think he is not," Serena rose. "And I must be at the theater."

"And I must meet my friend," Lord Ashmore said. He smiled at Serena and then his gaze grew intense. "Good God!" he exclaimed, "I would not have credited it. Have you ever essayed the role of an Indian princess, Miss Spencer?"

"An Indian princess, my lord?" she asked confusedly.

He nodded. "I have had the honor of meeting several . . . I am thinking mainly of the daughter of the Maharajah of Baroda, a tall, stately young woman in a glowing gold and turquoise sari. Her coloring was similar to yours, though you have much the advantage of her in looks."

"Oh, my lord, you are kind to say so," Serena murmured.

"I am not being kind," he assured her. "It is a most striking resemblance. There are some strikingly beautiful women in India and many of your coloring."

"Oh, my lord, I am complimented," Serena said softly.

"Papa, I think you are right," Arabella agreed enthusiastically. "I have seen paintings of girls from India, but I think Serena is even prettier than they are."

"Gracious, my head will be completely turned!" Serena smiled. "But, please, my lord, you have said you are in a hurry, and I must be at the theater."

"And shall be soon, Miss Spencer." He turned to Arabella. "Good night, my dear." Offering his arm to Serena, he hurriedly escorted her from the room.

Closing the door behind them, Arabella leaned against it, wishing she might have pulled it open and run after them, demanding to accompany Serena to the theater. If her father had not had a prior engagement, he could have brought her home. He could also have taken Serena to her lodgings. Unlike his sister, he appeared to approve of her. She sighed as she considered the real reason she had hoped to go to the theater. Julian, of course. Quite truthfully, she would have gone anywhere were she promised a meeting or even a glimpse of him.

On this night, however, she would play a game or two of piquet with her aunt and go to bed—just as if she, too, were a maiden lady. And would that be such a horrid fate if you could not marry the man you loved?

"Imagine," a delighted Arabella said to Lady Olivia as on a morning two days after Serena's visit they hurried up the boardwalk bound for the lending library, "Papa's saying that we may go to Reading so that I need not say farewell to Serena immediately. Was that not kind of him?"

Lady Olivia had been looking thoughtful, and that expression remained as she replied, "Yes, Adrian has been most accommodating of late."

"And," Arabella said triumphantly, "he thinks I should continue my friendship with Serena. *He* approves of her."

"That is quite obvious," Lady Olivia said dryly.

"And you still do not?" Arabella frowned.

"I do not *what*, my dear?"

"I am sure you understand my meaning, Aunt. You still do not approve of Serena. You have formed an opinion of her and it will not change, even though that same opinion was formed when first you met her and now she is grown up."

Lady Olivia did not answer immediately. Finally, she said, slowly, "Characters do not change."

"Well, then," Arabella asked edgily, "what is there about Serena's character that does not please you?"

"I admire frankness. I never feel that Serena is frank. To me, there is now and has always been an air of secretiveness about her."

"Oh, nonsense," Arabella scoffed. "I know her better than you and I tell you that she is frank and honest. I do not believe there is a secretive bone in her body."

"I pray that I am wrong," Lady Olivia said slowly. "I would rather be wrong than see you disappointed."

"I will never be disappointed by Serena," Arabella said strongly.

"Have you forgotten the fact that you have neither seen nor heard from her until very recently?" Lady Olivia inquired.

"She has explained that to my satisfaction," Arabella said after a slight hesitation

"I am delighted to hear it."

There was a note in her aunt's voice that moved Arabella to reply, "If you do not enjoy her company, at least you will enjoy the journey to Reading, will you not? Have you ever been there before?"

"I have passed through on the way to other places. Actually, a friend moved there, and I visited her once or twice."

"Ah, then, you must make a point of doing so again."

"No, she is no longer there. She was a widow, but she has married again and now lives in York."

Arabella was suddenly aware of confidences held back. However, she did not press her aunt for further information. Had there been someone she loved living in that same house where her friend had dwelled? It had always surprised her that, dowry or no dowry, her beautiful aunt had not married. At thirty-three, she still seemed much younger than her years, but there was an air of settled melancholy about her that hinted at buried secrets, and obviously she was not looking forward to their coming journey to Reading. She felt sorry for Lady Olivia, guessing that she longed to return home to their ancient house, located just outside Boston, in Lincolnshire. Obviously, she felt more comfortable there . . . and again her thoughts strayed to Reading. Had the friend had a brother and had the brother been in love with her aunt only to lose interest after the change in fortunes that had robbed her of her dowry and sent her brother to seek his fortune in India? And was she herself destined to become another Olivia because of her own unrequited passion for a man who was not only socially unacceptable but who had not the slightest interest in her?

She said, "The lending library is farther than I had imagined."

"Yes." Lady Olivia nodded. "However, it is well-stocked and has the newest volumes. I hope we find something to equal it in Reading."

"I wish we might be closer to the ocean in

Reading," Arabella said. "It is delightful to have the sea winds here and . . . Oh, dear!" She broke off as Lord Kinnard strode up to them, his broad face pink with sunburn. He was smiling at her quite as if her father had never strongly discouraged his suit.

"Ah," he said punctiliously bowing over her aunt's fingers before pressing a kiss on Arabella's unwillingly outstretched hand.

"How very pleasant to see you, Lady Olivia, and you, Lady Arabella." He glanced down at the books both ladies were carrying. "You are bound for the circulating library, no doubt. May I have the pleasure of walking with you?"

"If you choose," Lady Olivia said in a tone that neither welcomed nor dismissed him.

Arabella merely nodded, wishing him across the stretch of water before them—in Calais or even Rome!

"I was much surprised to see Lord Ashmore with that female who flaunts herself in the theater," Lord Kinnard remarked.

Arabella tensed. "If you are referring to Miss Spencer, my lord, I must tell you that we have been friends since childhood. She comes from an excellent family, but one that has suffered sad reverses, obliging her to work for her living."

"I cannot imagine anyone from a so-called 'good' family passing through the portals of a theater," he responded coldly. "Rogues and vagabonds all!"

"That is a phrase that dates from Shakespeare's day," Arabella dared to reply. "It is hardly applicable now, when some actresses have married nobles and *one* having been closely allied with the Royal family."

"I prefer not to discuss such shocking moral lapses," he said coldly. "I understand that you are soon leaving. May I hope that we will meet in London, Lady Arabella?''

"I do not know if we are going to London,'' Arabella replied.

"No, I suppose it were better to confer with your father as to your destination,'' Lord Kinnard responded.

"Yes, he will know,'' Lady Olivia said, thus preventing her niece from giving him the set-down trembling on her tongue.

"Very well, I will make it a point to ask him. Ah, there is the library, I will wish you good morning, my ladies.''

"Good morning, Lord Kinnard,'' Arabella said. "Oh,'' she added as he was lost to sight among the crowds, "I do dislike him.''

"I am surprised that he is not aware of your feelings, my dear, since you have not troubled to hide them. He is extremely thick-skinned.''

"Indeed, he is. Were I not sure that he is wealthy, I would assume that his pockets were to let and he was angling after my dowry.''

"My love.'' Lady Olivia came to a dead stop. "You do yourself a great disservice by that remark. He and every other gentleman who has so ardently pursued you is taken by your beauty and your sweetness of character—as well as your intelligence. I think you know that and in knowing it do not need to seek for compliments.''

"I was not,'' Arabella said crossly. "What can I do to prove to Lord Kinnard that I am not interested in him? Papa has told him that I am not interested in being married to him. I vow, he must have the hide of an elephant.''

"Ah, I am glad *they* did not meet,'' Lady Olivia said obscurely.

"What can you mean, Aunt?"

Lady Olivia lowered her voice. "Look to your left and you will see. A quick glance will serve."

Arabella obediently followed her aunt's instructions and tensed. "Mr. Sherlay," she murmured.

"The same." Lady Olivia nodded.

He was coming toward them, but he seemed to be deep in thought and he might have passed them had not Lady Olivia said graciously, "Mr. Sherlay, good morning."

He had been frowning, but his brow cleared as he saw them. "Good morning." He glanced at the books both ladies were carrying. "You must be going to the library. I am just returning."

"I am glad you are punctilious about taking back your books, especially since the company is due to move out," Lady Olivia said admiringly.

"I am moving out a little earlier," he explained. "I will be leaving as soon as I fetch my luggage from my lodgings."

"Oh, I thought that you would be performing Romeo tonight," Arabella said.

He shook his head. "The role will be taken by Mr. Stapely, who is usually Benvolio. He will also perform the role of Charles Surface when the company reaches Reading. I will be joining it there for the second Romeo."

"Oh, dear, I hope you have not had grave news from home," Lady Olivia said.

"No, it is not grave. I have been told that my uncle is back from a long journey. He wants to see me."

"Well, then, we shall certainly miss your Romeo and your Surface," Lady Olivia said regretfully, "but you will surely be back before we leave."

"Am I to infer that you are going to Reading?" he asked.

"Yes." Arabella smiled. "Papa has told me that since I have not seen Serena for such a long time, he thinks we should have a greater opportunity to be together before we return to Lincolnshire."

"I see." There was a slight frown in his eyes as he continued, "That is certainly very considerate of Lord Ashmore."

"He has always been most considerate," Arabella said warmly. "I mean, whenever it is possible. He has been away so often and for years at a time."

"Oh, indeed?" Mr. Sherlay's dark gaze had become peculiarly intent. "He is a traveler, then?"

"Only to India," Arabella explained. "Papa was involved in importing and exporting."

"I see. But not anymore?"

"No, my brother has decided to shake the dust of foreign shores from his boots and settle down in Lincolnshire. We live outside of Stow," Lady Olivia explained.

"I see." He nodded. "There are parts of Lincolnshire that are very beautiful."

"I must agree with you," Lady Olivia said.

It seemed to Arabella that Mr. Sherlay was on the verge of saying something more, but evidently he thought better of it for with a brief smile, he said merely, "I must be going. I will need as much of the daylight as possible if I am to complete the first stage of my journey before nightfall."

"I do wish you good weather, Mr. Sherlay," Arabella said.

He gave her a brief smile. "I thank you, Lady Arabella."

"I wish you the same," Lady Olivia told him.

He murmured his thanks again and then hurried away.

"Oh, he is charming and so well-spoken," Arabella said.

"Indeed he is. And with none of the affectation that often colors the speech of those who are in his profession," Lady Olivia said thoughtfully.

"What a pity he is leaving. Serena will be desolated." Arabella sighed.

"He is not leaving forever, my dear," Lady Olivia responded crisply. "Come, we must get to the library and back—we have more packing to do."

Arabell did not immediately obey her aunt. She stood watching Mr. Sherlay as he strode up the boardwalk, becoming lost among the crowds all too quickly and leaving her with a hollow feeling inside that she certainly should not have been experiencing, particularly since he was devoted to her best friend. Unfortunately, she was fast learning that she was very envious of that same best friend and that she wished most fervently something might occur to separate Serena and her Julian—that she might have the comforting of that disconsolate young man. A moment later, she banished thoughts that were both disloyal and unworthy of her. She did love Serena and she wanted the best for her dearest friend—and the best, of course, was Mr. Julian Sherlay.

5

Reading was a change from Brighton—not nearly so pretty, but the theater was large, and according to Mr. Soames, the actor who played small roles and doubled as an advance man for the Gordon troupe, there was an audience eagerly awaiting the company.

Much to Arabella's disappointment, Lord Ashmore had booked them into the Bell on the outskirts of the town, a goodly distance from the theater and from the inn where most of the actors were staying, Serena included. He had apologized for that, explaining that there was a fair in progress near the city and that all the other inns were fully booked. He had subsequently chided his daughter for being so downcast. "You will be able to see your friend, Serena. I myself will bring her to the Bell . . . a belle to the Bell." He had laughed at his little witticism.

Arabella had laughed, too, but only dutifully. Naturally, she could not tell her father that she had entertained hopes of walking down the street with her aunt or Lizzie and happening to pass the theater. There was always, she had reasoned, a chance that she might meet Julian Sherlay. He had returned earlier than he had anticipated and had, in fact, been in time to thrill audiences as Romeo in the company's initial presentation of the play. She had missed him

even more than she anticipated, and not even the
presence of Serena, brought to the inn as her father
had promised, compensated for his loss—if she could
call it by so large a word.

During Serena's visits, which had numbered only
three and were brief because of her commitments at
the theater, she had not dared introduce his name
lest her friend believe she was showing far too much
interest in him. And with Julian's image in mind, she
found herself regrettably less interested in their
conversations, especially since Serena's main subject
was her growing dissatisfaction with her work in the
theater. Indeed, they had come close to having words
of that.

"I would give anything to be in your place,"
Arabella had said during Serena's last visit.

"And I would give anything to have you there,"
Serena had snapped. "Then you could know first-
hand the so-called joys of being an actress. My poor
child, you are such an innocent. You speak as if the
theater were a palace and actors the kings and queens
they portray on stage. You know nothing about
dreary lodgings and the way innkeepers look at
you—as if you were the dregs of humanity. You are
treated with contempt and . . . Oh, why go on? You
will never understand me. You still want to act.
However, what you call acting would not get you the
role of a chambermaid with half a line to speak."

Hurt had set Arabella's throat to throbbing. "At
school . . ." she had begun, foolishly in the circumstances.

"School?" Serena's laugh had been unpleasant.
"You were certainly the most talented pupil in
school, but that *was* school and this is the world. And
. . ." She had paused and then said, "Oh, Arabella,

my dear, what am I saying? You were a good actress and I am wronging you. It is only that I do hate the theater. I hate the traveling from place to place. I hate being cold in winter and too hot in summer. I hate rising while it is still dark so that we might be on our way to our next engagement. I want to be comfortable and peaceful and happy. I would trade my soul for that."

She had been very sorry for Serena—so sorry that she had managed to overlook the harsh words she had leveled at herself. They had stung, and the sting had not been quite obliterated by her apology. However, later, after she had gone, Arabella had found she could forgive her completely. She was sure that Serena was probably much criticized by her fellow actors for her lackluster performances. It was possible, too, that she might be in danger of losing her position—and then, what would she do? Marry Julian? Probably. Arabella winced and moved restively.

"Please, milady," Lizzie protested. "Yer wrigglin' about so I cannot fasten these pesky hooks."

"Oh, Lizzie, I am sorry." Arabella obediently stood still. She was dressing for the second performance of *Romeo and Juliet*, scheduled during the company's second week in the town. She must be careful to greet Serena warmly when she went back to the greenroom. Furthermore, she must not wax over-enthusiastic about seeing the performance and, more to the point, she had best not single out Mr. Sherlay and praise his performance above all others or Serena might guess her secret.

A tap on the door scattered Arabella's thoughts. "Yes," she called.

Lord Ashmore opened the door a crack. "Are you

nearly finished dressing, my dear?'' he asked a trifle edgily.

"Yes, very nearly, Papa. Lizzie is just buttoning my gown."

"Ah, very good, my dear. We must not be late, you know."

"I do not see how we can be late, for we will be there a good hour before the performance," she said in some surprise.

"We must always allow for possible accidents on the road."

"But it is not a very long road," she returned, but found herself speaking to air, for Lord Ashmore had already closed her door.

Arabella smiled. Her father was in a very good mood of late. In fact, she had never seen him quite so ebullient. Even her aunt had remarked about it. "He has something on his mind that is pleasing him, something that he is not minded to confide—as yet."

"I wonder what it could be?" Arabella had asked.

"He will tell us when he has a mind to do so. He has always kept his own counsel. It used to make me very cross when I was little. 'I've got a secret, Livia,' he'd say, and I would beg and beg him to tell me what it might be and he would only look mysterious and say, 'When the time is ripe, you will know.' The time was never ripe on time, I used to think.' "

"Have you any idea what it might be now, Aunt?" Arabella had asked.

"I cannot imagine." Lady Olivia had shrugged.

"And nor can I imagine," Arabella said to herself.

"Do stand still, milady," Lizzie protested. "Yer wigglin' so that I missed a buttonhole."

"Sorry, Lizzie," Arabella murmured, and

obediently stood stiffly while Lizzie continued with her task. Then, as she pushed the last button through its ho'e, there was another tap on her door. ''Yes?'' she called.

Lady Olivia opened the door. She was looking quite lovely in a blue lutestring, and she also looked amazingly young. However, she was not old, she was only thirty-three; in fourteen years, she, Arabella, would be thirty-three and, she thought desolately, unmarried, for having met the only man she could ever love, she wanted no other. She would be a companion to her father, who had also loved only once and lost his bride within a year of their marriage.

''A penny for your thoughts, my dear?'' Lady Olivia asked. ''You are looking unexpectedly gloomy.''

Arabella gave her a startled look. ''I vow that they are worth less than a groat,'' she managed to say lightly. ''Is it time to leave for the theater?''

''It is time and past, according to your father, who is already out by the coach.''

''He does seem to be in a hurry tonight,'' Arabella commented with a laugh.

''Indeed, yes. I have never known him so impatient.''

''Do I scent a mystery?'' Arabella asked.

''I do,'' her aunt said frankly.

''I wonder what it might be. I expect we'll know about it presently.''

''I hope so.'' Lady Olivia smiled.

''Well, arriving at the theater early will give me more time to spend with Serena,'' Arabella commented.

"Considering your great friendship, it would have seemed to me that she would have made more of an effort to see you," Lady Olivia said tartly.

"Will you always criticize her?" Arabella frowned.

"As long as she makes it so easy for me to criticize her, I expect I will."

Arabella refrained from commenting. Comments and arguments were futile when it came to Serena. Her aunt would never like her, and of course, that did not matter, since once they had left Reading, it was quite possible that years would pass before they met again. Arabella sighed and flushed, realizing that she was not really thinking of Serena when she envisioned that leave-taking.

Lord Ashmore deposited his "fair ladies," as he called them, at the stage door a few minutes before seven and surprised them with the announcement that he had an appointment nearby and might not be able to join them until after the performance started.

Coming into the stage entrance, Arabella asked for Serena and was considerably disappointed to learn that she had been suddenly taken ill and had returned to her boardinghouse.

"She left ye the tickets, milady," the custodian said, producing them.

"Oh, dear, I hope it is nothing serious," Arabella said worriedly. "Is she very ill?"

"I'd not be knowin', yer ladyship," he mumbled.

"Well"—Arabella brightened slightly—"we will be seeing Mr. Sherlay. I do love his Romeo, do not you, Aunt Olivia?"

"How many times must I tell you that I do." Lady Olivia smiled. "He is a very fine actor, and furthermore, he was an air of refinemeent that helps his portrayal immeasurably. Indeed, he could easily be a

Veronese nobleman, which is more than I can say for most actors. Generally, they are a shock when you meet them off stage without costumes, makeup, and footlights at their feet.''

"That might be true, except in the case of Serena,'' Arabella said loyally.

"But, my dearest,'' Lady Olivia drawled, ''I thought we were in agreement regarding her acting ability.'' She added, ''Come, let us go to the front of the theater.''

"You still do not like Serena,'' Arabella commented as they found their seats.

"No,'' Lady Olivia said frankly. ''I cannot say that I do. Your father, however, seems to admire her. That ought to satisfy you. He will not cavil at inviting her to our home, should you wish to extend such an invitation to her.''

"If you would try to know her better . . .''

"My dear''—Lady Olivia scanned the playbill she held in her hand—''I know her quite as well as I wish to know her. I am sure that I have friends whom you do not enjoy.''

"But why—'' Arabella began.

"Shall I say,'' Lady Olivia interrupted, ''that I do not find her frank and open. There is something secretive about her. I have been more aware of that quality in these last weeks than ever before. But I beg that we do not dwell on her. Let us prepare to enjoy the play and be glad that we will soon have the pleasure of Mr. Sherlay's truly excellent Romeo.''

"Ah!'' Arabella brightened. ''I am very glad about that.''

The applause was loud and the actors were recalled again and again

Arabella said defiantly, ''I do not care if there is a carriage awaiting us. I must go back and congratulate Mr. Sherlay.'' She brought a handkerchief to eyes still tearing from emotions roused by Romeo's poisoned demise and by Juliet's passing, too. Mrs. Gordon had surpassed herself tonight. She had seemed amazingly young and vulnerable, and to Arabella's mind her performance had received its fire from her Romeo's riveting delineation. Certainly, she must have been gladdened by his return.

''Very well, my dear, I will accompany you, of course.'' Lady Olivia frowned. ''I cannot understand Adrian. He said nothing of an appointment that must keep him occupied through most of the night.'' She stared down at the note that had come by messenger and had been handed to her during the interval by one of the ushers.

''Alas, our mystery remains unsolved.'' Arabella smiled. ''Do let us go back and see Mr. Sherlay. Perhaps Serena will be recovered by now and she will be with him.''

As usual, the greenroom was crowded, but still it was possible to see that Julian was alone, smiling nervously at the applause he had just received from a group of people currently surrounding him. There was a lack, however, of the ogling gallants who were wont to come and raise their quizzing glasses at the leading actresses. Those girls who had appeared in the dances of the first act had left early, and neither had been blessed with the sort of beauty that characterized Serena. Had she been present, Arabella thought, there would be no lack of ogling gentlemen, and again she wondered anxiously about the malady that had felled her. She was truly disappointed at not seeing her—and for reasons she had not confided to

her aunt. Of late, it had seemed to Arabella that
Serena was being less than frank with her. In fact,
she seemed to have something on her mind that she
wanted to confide, but had not confided because . . .

"My love," Lady Olivia said edgily, "now is not
the time to fall into deep thought. Let us greet Mr.
Sherlay and be gone."

"Oh, dear," Arabella murmured contritely, "I am
sorry."

As she and her aunt started to make their way to
Julian's side, he saw them and in another moment
had deftly separated himself from several admiring
females and came to them to be greeted with
restrained but heartfelt enthusiasm by Lady Olivia
and with fervor by Arabella, who again—or, rather,
as usual whenever she was in his company—felt her
pulses stirring and a pounding in her throat. She also
had the confusing sensation that each separate part of
her body was throbbing to a different rhythm.
Furthermore, her cheeks were burning and her
breath was coming fast. She felt, indeed, as if she had
been running, and it was with difficulty that she
uttered her congratulations.

He looked gratified, but still she had a feeling that
he was not quite aware of what she was telling him.
She understood that. He was not quite down from
the heights of performing Romeo. The mantle of actor
had not yet dropped from his shoulders. His heartfelt, heartbreaking demise still clouded his mind and
with it, she did not doubt, was his possible concern
over the absence of Serena, who was wont to stand at
his side at such times.

Belatedly, she recalled the report of her friend's
illness and now, suddenly, she did not quite believe
in it. She did not know why she was entertaining

these doubts . . . No, that was not quite true. They were based on what she now recognized as a definite evasiveness on the part of Serena.

Almost without volition, she said, "I had hoped that Serena would have recovered from her indisposition by now. I hope she will be better soon."

He regarded her quizzically. "I hope so, too," he said after a brief pause. "You and Lady Olivia are alone here tonight?"

"Yes, Papa was not able to join us. He had an appointment."

"I see . . ." he began, and at that moment was approached by another group of people all warmly uttering their congratulations.

Arabella moved away and, looking around for her aunt, saw her across the room speaking with Mr. Gordon. She started toward her, only to find her way blocked by a tall, husky young man who grinned down at her in far too familiar a manner while he put a large hand on her shoulder.

"Well, my pretty, I do not remember seeing you on the stage," he said jovially.

Arabella directed an annoyed look at him, wondering if she must have these experiences every time she was alone, however, briefly. "I am not a performer, sir," she said freezingly. "Please be good enough to take your hand from my shoulder."

He did not obey her. Instead, the pressure from his hand grew stronger. "I take it you are alone here. Why do we not repair to the tavern next door, my lovely?"

"I am with my aunt, sir. Now if you will please . . ."

"Ah, your aunt." He nodded and smiled. "And

how much does she usually demand for your services?''

"My services?'' Arabella repeated confusedly. "I think you must be mad.'' She tried to twist away from a hold that was fast becoming hurtful. Scanning the crowded room, she no longer saw Lady Olivia. She looked toward Julian, but did not see him either. She glared up at the man beside her. "I must ask you again, sir, to let me go,'' she said in the ringing tones she had used when playing Petruchio and other roles at school. "You are under a strong misapprehension. I am not alone here. I am not . . .''

His laughter drowned out her protests. "I do not care what you are not, my beautiful. You must tell your aunt that I am willing to pay your price and . . . Ooff!'' He suddenly went reeling back, a hand to his mouth, as Julian, his arm around Arabella's shoulders, said coldly, "I will thank you to cease annoying this young lady. Jim,'' he called. "Throw this person out of here, if you will. He is making a great nuisance of himself.''

The man, glaring at Julian, yelled, "I'll have you know, damn your eyes, you rogue, that I am Sir Harry Boulton!''

"I do not care who you are, sir,'' Julian said icily. "You have been making yourself obnoxious to Lady Ashmore and—''

"A lady, is she?'' Sir Harry growled. "A lady, alone and casting her eyes about—''

"Jim,'' Julian called a second time as a tall burly individual made his way through a suddenly silent greenroom. "Take that man out, please.''

Sir Harry, looking up at the man called Jim towering over him, said, "If you so much as touch me, I'll have the law on you. I will have this whole damned company in chains.''

"I won't touch you, sir, providin' that you comes wi' me peacefullike," Jim responded in a surprisingly gentle tone of voice.

"I'll . . . You'll hear more about this, the lot of you," Sir Harry growled, and turning on his heel, he lurched out.

Arabella raised grateful eyes to Mr. Sherlay's face. "I am sorry," she said unhappily. "I mean, I do thank you, but I would not have made trouble for you and the company for the world."

"I am sure that you have not, my dear Lady Arabella," he said soothingly. "I hope he did not hurt you."

"Oh, no, he was just h-horrid," she explained with a little shudder. "He spoke about my services and said I must come to the tavern with him."

"Damn the lout," he snapped. "Anyone can see that you are an innocent." He was looking at her, Arabella thought confusedly, as if he were seeing her for the first time. Then, he said abruptly, "Where is your aunt, my dear? Why are you not with her?"

"She was here a moment ago. I was looking in another direction, and when I turned back, he was there and I could not see her. She was with Mr. Gordon."

"Ah, and probably still is. I will find her and take you to her."

"Oh, I do thank you, Mr. Sherlay," she said gratefully. She continued anxiously, "Are you sure that that man will not make trouble for you?"

"I think that if he tries to do so, the fact that he was trying to ensnare a young and titled member of our audience will weigh in our favor."

"If he brings the matter before a constable, he will need more than your word. I will write a deposition explaining what took place. I think I had best do it immediately."

"Perhaps that is advisable, milady," he said. "And I do thank you for the suggestion. I might not have thought of it myself. Come, then, let us see if we can find your aunt . . ." He scanned the crowds. "Ah, I see her. She *is* still with Mr. Gordon."

Informed of the circumstances requiring her niece's deposition, Lady Olivia readily agreed that it must be written, and a worried Mr. Gordon expressed his thanks several times. "People are touchy," he sighed. "And the man being titled . . . Actors, you know, count for naught."

"You will need witnesses," Lady Olivia said. "I will write a deposition to that effect."

"You were not there," Arabella protested.

"There's none to know I was not," her aunt answered equably. "I am tall enough to have seen my niece struggling in the arms of her captor and to have been prevented from hurrying to her side by the crowds in the greenroom."

"You are most kind, milady," Mr. Gordon said warmly. "And you, too, Lady Arabella."

"It is the least I can do for all the pleasure I have received from your performances, sir." Her eyes rested briefly on Julian's face, but he was not looking at her. He was staring into the distance, and judging by the frown between his brows, he was not happy. Probably he was still brooding over Serena's absence, and quite suddenly, Arabella was very angry with her friend for yielding to what she guessed must be a slight indisposition. Had she, Arabella, been bedded by a quinsy, she would have arisen from her couch and come to see the man she loved in his performance. Indeed, she would not have missed a single one even if she could not take part in them. Serena did not value Julian Sherlay's love highly enough. Were she in her friend's place . . . But it was useless to indulge in wishful thinking.

Too many barriers rose between them and the greatest barrier of all was, of course, that he was not the least interested in her. Once more, she looked up at him and again failed to meet his eyes. They were fixed on some distant point . . . They were fixed rather, on an image that lurked behind them . . . on Serena, unfortunately absent but, in essence, here.

"Let us sign the deposition and have done," she said almost brusquely. "I think it were time we returned to the inn."

"Of course, my dear Lady Arabella," Mr. Sherlay said. "You are most kind."

His attention was finally fixed on her, and conversely Arabella wished it were not, since she read only a polite and impersonal gratitude in his gaze.

"But where could my brother had gone, Mr. Sims?" Lady Olivia, standing in the parlor of the Bell Inn, was speaking to the innkeeper, her eyes dark with anxiety. "My brother left you no word as to when he would return this morning? And why was I not informed of his absence last night, pray?"

The innkeeper, nervously pleating his apron, turned a confused gaze on her. His full round face was a mask of anxiety. "We only got the word this morning, milady."

"Well, I must say I find it passing strange," she

said tartly. "At least he might have specified a time when he meant to return."

Listening to this exchange, Arabella, standing near her aunt, felt a concern bordering on fright. It was nearly eleven in the morning, and despite his message that he would be back before noon, the time being dependent on the matter at hand, there might be other ominous reasons for his failure to return. There were highwaymen aplenty on the roads, and since the mysterious errand he had mentioned had required nighttime travel, he could easily have been held up. Though his coachman and the postboy were handy with guns, highwaymen sometimes traveled in gangs. She looked at her aunt's set face and guessed that much the same fears were coursing through her mind.

And furthermore . . . Her thoughts came to an abrupt end as the front door of the hostelry was suddenly thrust open by Lizzie, who darted inside, her eyes wide. "Ohhhh, milady," she shrilled, looking from Lady Olivia to Arabella.

"Good God, child, what's amiss?" Lady Olivia cried.

"Oh, milady." The abigail shook her head. "I do not know . . . I do not know what to s-say."

"But what is it, Lizzie?" Arabella demanded impatiently, thinking that the girl had the look of someone bursting with news.

Hard on this conclusion, Lord Ashmore strode in, but he was not alone. With him was a blushing and apparently ecstatic Serena, clutching his arm and looking from Arabella to her aunt, half-shyly, half-triumphantly.

"Serena," Arabella exclaimed. "What—"

"My dears," Lord Ashmore interrupted, "I wish you to greet the lady who yesterday, by way of a special license, became my wife."

Lady Olivia tensed and the color drained from her cheeks as she said, "You . . . you cannot be serious, Adrian." In that same moment, she received a lightning glance from the bride.

"Oh, Serena," Arabella cried. "Oh, I am delighted . . . Oh, dear, dear Serena and Papa, I am so happy for you . . . for you both. Oh, how entirely lovely!" Moving to Serena, she flung her arms around her friend, kissing her. Then, moving to her father, she kissed him, too, saying, "How wonderful!" Then, suddenly, she laughed as she looked at Serena. "But I cannot, I will not call you *mother*!"

"No, silly, of course, you cannot." Serena seemed caught between laughter and tears. "We will be sisters, of course."

"Sisters, of course," Arabella echoed. "Oh, how lovely, how very lovely!"

Lord Ashmore fastened an approving look on his daughter. "I knew you must welcome her, my dear." He did not look at his sister. His gaze had returned to the face of his beautiful young bride.

Even in the midst of her excitement and her all-abiding happiness for Serena and her father, Arabella was uncomfortably aware of the silent presence of her aunt, and in her mind's eye, she could also see Julian Sherlay. Both would be similarly unhappy. Indeed, a quick glance at Lady Olivia showed her that she was standing as still as a statue, all animation drained from her countenance. Indeed, her features might have been carved from marble. And would Julian, upon receiving the news, look the same. She was uncomfortably positive that he would.

The flurry of congratulations was at an end, and Serena was sitting in Arabella's chamber while Lord Ashmore made arrangements for their immediate departure.

Arabella had been listening to her friend's account of how she had fallen in love with Lord Ashmore and he with her; and now, as Serena finished speaking, she said, "Will you go to the theater to bid farewell to the company?"

Serena was silent a moment. Then she shook her head, saying with a slight chill in her tones, "I have written expressing my thanks for their kindness. I have also sent a note to Julian." She fixed her eyes on Arabella's face, adding, "I knew you had it in mind to ask me about him."

Arabella nodded. "I do think you ought to have told him about your marriage in person, since he is so very much in love with you."

Serena was silent a moment before saying, "I hope you have not seen fit to make that observation to your father, my dear."

Arabella tensed, hearing a surprisingly unfriendly note in Serena's voice. In that moment, she could not remember if she had spoken to her father about Julian and Serena or not. However, discretion being the better part of valor, she said, "No, we have not discussed it."

She was rewarded by a brief smile from Serena. "I had forgotten how closemouthed you can be on occasion. And truly, Arabella, I feel you might be overanxious as to how Julian will receive the knowledge of my marriage."

Despite her words, Arabella read anxiety in her friend's gaze. She hesitated, but could not help saying, "I fear that he will be extremely upset."

"Undoubtedly, he will." Serena shrugged. "However, he will not go into prolonged mourning, I can assure you. I am not the first nor will I be the last of the females to whom Julian has presented a piece of his heart. Indeed, if it were more than a mere figure of speech, he would not have a heart left."

Serena had spoken lightly, and against her will, Arabella found herself resenting that attitude. She would never have suspected Serena of having a cruel streak in her nature, but certainly she was being unnecessarily cruel and also unfair to poor Julian, who was so obviously in love with her.

She contented herself, however, with saying coolly, "It did not appear that way to me."

"My dear Arabella"—Serena's smile was mocking, even derisive—"what do you know of gentlemen, you with your sheltered, becastled existence? You do remember MacHeath's ballad in *The Beggar's Opera*? 'How happy I would be with either, were t'other dear charmer away?' Julian has played that role often. It is one of his best impersonations. He plays it with gusto and with a thorough knowledge of MacHeath's character, gained through experience not imagination."

A series of images traveled through Arabella's mind: Julian looking at Serena with his heart in his eyes, he smiling at her friend as they took their curtain calls, he pushing her forward to accept the weak applause of a disinterested audience, an audience interested only in himself. She had a strong notion that her friend was lying to herself as well as to her, but now was not the time to argue. She said merely, "I do hope that you are right, Serena."

"Of course I am," Serena said bracingly. "And I love your father, you know I think I loved him at first sight, and he has told me that as soon as he first saw me, he, too, could think of nothing else.''

A look at Serena's softened expression, her shining eyes and her general air of ecstacy, Arabella was sure that she must be speaking the truth . . . mainly because she had absolutely no talent for acting.

6

At intervals during the journey to Ashmore Hold —the sprawling Tudor mansion her family had lived in for almost three hundred years, the house having been built during the reign of Mary I— Arabella gave Serena bits and pieces of the history of the family of which she had just become a member, and of the house itself. More information trembled on her lips as the coach rounded the last bend in the long road leading to the hold. However, in view of Serena's almost palpable and, to her mind, surprising excitement, she said nothing. She had been unprepared for her friend's ecstatic reaction to the long driveway and the vast house with its surrounding gardens. It was not the first time she had seen it, certainly. She had been a guest here on numerous occasions during their years at school.

"But there it is, the ruined tower!" Serena suddenly cried. "Destroyed under . . ."

"Northumberland's forces," Arabella said.

"Yes, yes, I do remember," Serena breathed. "Your ancestor was loyal to Mary, the eldest daughter of Henry VIII and actually supported her claim to the throne for all he was a Protestant."

"He knew her when they were children," Arabella nodded.

"I remember that, too. You told me she was an unhappy little girl."

"Yes, she was separated from her mother—"

"Katherine of Aragon," Serena put in quickly. "And after Mary died, he transferred his loyalty to Elizabeth."

"It was not really a transference," Arabella corrected. "He had always liked Elizabeth, too."

"I call that very diplomatic," Serena smiled. "And he entertained her Majesty here . . . Oh, I must see that marvelous portrait again."

"You'll be seeing her Majesty's portrait quite often, I'm thinking," Arabella said implishly. She winked at Serena.

She received no answering wink in return. "I know . . . oh, I can hardly wait to see it again, and all the other wonderful rooms." Serena fell silent.

"We feel the same way. We are always glad to come home again," Arabella said and was immediately sorry she had included her aunt in that comment. She visited a quick look on Lady Olivia's face and looked away as quickly. Her aunt was sitting next to her, one hand on the strap at her side and the other in her lap. Generally, her eyes had been fixed on the passing scenery and seemingly she was unaware of the chill glances directed at her by the bride. Yet, despite her silence, she was an uncomfortable presence and bid fair to remain so, once they were home. She had not troubled to volunteer any information about her new home to Serena, but as they rounded the road and glimpsed the house rising through the trees, Arabella had seen a look of pain on her face. She found herself half-annoyed, half-sorry for Lady Olivia's unrelenting dislike of Serena. The idea of the four of them living together even in the commodious reaches of the hold seemed unthinkable, and even as that thought crossed her mind, her aunt corroborated those feelings.

"I have written to Lady Cavendish, my friend in London, telling her that I have at last decided to take advantage of her long-standing invitation to come to the city."

Serena, giving her a quick glance, said, "Oh, when will you be leaving us, Lady Olivia?"

The question was uttered quietly but with an eagerness that was unmistakable.

Without giving Serena the benefit of a direct answer, Lady Olivia continued speaking to her niece as she had done whenever possible throughout the journey. "I will be going as soon as I have gathered my belongings."

"Oh, Aunt Olivia," Arabella said impulsively, "I do wish you might remain a little longer."

She was aware of a quelling stare from Serena, who in a chill voice said, "I am sure that Lady Olivia must be anxious to leave."

"You are quite right, Serena." Lady Olivia fixed a glacial look on her. "I have long been looking forward to visiting my friend and I believe that a new-made bride must have time to become accustomed to her surroundings."

"Oh, perhaps I ought to go with you," Arabella said quickly.

"You would be most welcome, my dear."

"No," Serena protested. She fixed pleading eyes on her friend's face. "Please, Arabella, you do not want to leave, do you?"

"Not if you wish me to stay, Serena," Arabella said with a fond smile.

"Oh, I do. I most certainly do," Serena said urgently.

It was an embarrassing moment but Lady Olivia said smoothly, "There, then it is all settled. I would imagine that I will leave within the week."

Serena made no comment. She was looking out the window and it was a few minutes later that she said, "Oh, the way to the house is truly beautiful."

"Yes," Arabella agreed, feeling . . . But she was not quite sure what she was feeling. No, that was not true. She really hated to think of her aunt leaving— and she wished strongly that Serena might have had the courtesy to underplay her evident pleasure at Lady Olivia's decision. Still, Serena was no actress and she certainly had no reason to be other than glad of Lady Olivia's departure.

Her aunt had not said very much on the journey from Reading. However, implicit in her silence were her feelings regarding what she must believe to be her brother's folly. In that same moment, Arabella was cognizant of a deep regret: so much in her life was changing and it had all happened in so brief a time. She was seized by a longing to stretch out her arms and hold Lady Olivia against her, begging her to stay, willing her to stay. Second thoughts, however, crowded in to assure her that she was being foolish. There was no reason for her aunt to remain. Her presence at the hold would only cause strife. She did wish, however, that Lady Olivia had kept her strong dislike for the bride to herself—but again, that would not have sufficed. Such a measure would have come far too late. Lady Olivia had never scrupled to

reveal her feelings concerning her friend, and Serena
had returned dislike for dislike.

All in all, it would be easier for them both with
Lady Olivia away. Serena would naturally believe
she deserved Arabella's loyalty and she would also
resent her great fondness for her aunt, might resent it
even now. She glanced at Serena but did not catch
her eye. Once more she was avidly staring out of the
window at the great house to which she was coming
as bride and as lady. Her excitement was obvious,
and why should it not be? Serena, more than anyone
she had ever known, needed the sort of security
that Lord Ashmore had given her—security, respectability, and a tranquil life. Given her great fondness for her friend, she could only be pleased that at
last she was receiving them.

On a chill November morning, nearly three months
after her return to the hold, Arabella awoke early
after a restless night filled with frightening dreams;
these, she realized as she opened her eyes, were the
extensions of the thoughts circulating through her
mind before falling asleep.

Now she lay looking at the ceiling, the familiar
ceiling in the chamber she had occupied ever since
she was old enough to leave the nursery. Her gaze
shifted to the windows, two facing the garden and
one a barrier of trees. Slipping out of bed, she moved
to the garden side and stared down at foliage,
autumn turned to red and gold. And at the end of
this month she, supposedly, would be bound to
London on her wedding journey and then to Paris.

She shuddered. The foliage blurred and the
remaining flowers were blurred with the rainbowed
glimmer of tears. She blinked them away. Tears did

not help. She had wept copiously when she had begged her father not to accept Lord Kinnard's offer of marriage.

"Please, I have told you so many, many times that I do not want to marry him. In Brighton, you told me that I need not wed him if I did not choose to do so. What has changed your mind?"

He had looked at her strangely, his gaze a mixture of anger and disappointment. "I am afraid that these little games of yours entertain no one but yourself, Arabella. I must beg that you have done."

"Games? I do not understand you, Papa," she had said confusedly.

He had given her an exasperated look. "You told Serena that you were only teasing him when you refused him. That was uncommonly cruel of you, Arabella. Indeed, I never expected that my daughter could be quite so perverse. I am deeply shocked."

She had stared at him incredulously. "I told Serena nothing of the sort. She is lying," she had accused furiously only to see her father's face pale and his eyes narrow. Before he could speak, however, she had continued, "She *is* lying. I told her more than once that I did not like Lord Kinnard, and now for her own peculiar reasons, she has seen fit to—"

He had raised his hand. "I do not wish to hear another word against my wife!" He had continued in fury-filled tones, "As long as I have known you, you have been singing her praises and now . . . now, you have turned against her like a serpent because out of sympathy for Lord Kinnard, she has seen fit to reveal your shoddy little tricks at his expense, teasing and flirting with him as if he did not have feelings. Well—"

"That is not true," she had interrupted.

"It is true. It is all too true. Serena has seen you do it. She told me that she begged you to please try to consider *his* feelings, and you told her that it was no concern of hers. She is at a loss to understand you, and so am I."

"And I am at a loss to understand her," Arabella had cried. "She knows full well that I dislike him."

"She knows nothing of the kind. I fear you speak out of two sides of your mouth, Arabella—or perhaps you have conveniently chosen to forget all the confidences you exchanged with her in Brighton, those gleeful confidences concerning the little games you were playing with Lord Kinnard. She has not forgotten them, and she thought it best that I be acquainted with your true state of mind."

"Serena imagines that she knows my true state of mind, Papa," Arabella had demanded sarcastically.

She ought not to have called Lord Ashmore "Papa," she thought bitterly. He no longer seemed to be her father. The man who had sat in the large carved chair at the desk in the library had seemed more like a judge facing a criminal.

"Enough of this," the stranger in her father's chair had said hastily. "These ugly little games must end. Your . . . my wife and I feel that you would have to look far and wide to find a man who loves you as Lord Kinnard loves you—a feeling, I might add, that your perverse actions certainly do not warrant. In fact—"

At that juncture she had tried to interrupt this man who looked like Lord Ashmore but who wore an expression she had never seen before, but he had raised a quelling hand.

"Let me have my say, Arabella," he had actually

thundered. "You are nearing your nineteenth
birthday and you are quite old enough to be wed.
Your poor mother was only seventeen when she
became my bride . . ." He had sighed and shaken his
head. "I never thought that I would be saying this,
but I am glad she did not live to learn of her
daughter's duplicity—she who never told a lie in all
her life! And if you do not love Lord Kinnard,
Arabella, you have given him ample reason to believe
that you do, and you will marry him. We have
decided, your . . . Serena and I, that the marriage will
take place in November. You are fortunate indeed to
have won the affections of this worthy and wealthy
young man. I might add that he has expressed a
desire to take you to London and subsequently to
Paris for your wedding trip."

"I do not wish to go as far as the end of the road
with him, Papa. I do not like him. I would rather
never be married than be married to him," she had
cried.

"That is not what you told Serena, my dear," he
had responded coldly. "And I might add that she
was most reluctant to betray your confidence and
would have held her peace had she not felt so sorry
for Lord Kinnard."

"So you have already said, Papa. And I say to you
that the only confidence on the subject of Lord
Kinnard that I ever gave to Serena was that I could
not bear him. If you do not want me here, Papa, say
so. Let me go to my aunt in London. I can stay with
her."

"No, Arabella, I wish to hear no more arguments
on this matter. I have already given my consent to the
son of my old and dearest friend."

"An old and dearest friend whom you've not seen

in years . . . a friend who died while you were still in India!''

"Arabella," Lord Ashmore had said coldly, "we are arguing at cross purposes. I have given my word and the wedding will take place as planned."

She had stared at him a long moment, reading determination in his cold gaze. Then, recognizing the folly of further argument, she had said, "Very well, Father, I will do as you ask."

He had not been surprised by her sudden capitulation, and thinking back on that, she guessed that he had taken it as an admission of guilt. He had said with obvious relief, "I am pleased that you have at last seen reason, my dear. I will tell Serena and I know that she will also be pleased."

"I am sure she will be, Papa," she had replied coldly and a touch sarcastically.

He had caught that inflection and frowned. He had started to say something, and then, obviously changing his mind, he had coolly dismissed her.

She had thought of going to Serena and confronting her with her lies, but a second thought had told her that it would be no use. Serena would go weeping to her husband and there would be another confrontation.

Now, as she stared into the garden, Arabella was once more going over the events of the last three months, trying to recall when the breach between herself and her erstwhile friend had first appeared, a tiny slit of a breach, growing wider and wider until Serena, overcome with anger and jealousy, had made her outrageous move, convincing first Lord Kinnard and then her father that she, Arabella, had been playing a deep game of "let's pretend."

"Why?" she whispered.

Moving away from her window, Arabella lay down on her bed again, mentally going over the series of events that had led up to her pending marriage. They flowed back into her mind's eyes and presently she began to realize just how and when she had managed to estrange her so-called best friend.

Her initial error, if so it could be termed, was her obvious unhappiness over Lady Olivia's decision to leave her brother's house. Serena had not immediately commented on that, but later it had been brought home to Arabella that she considered her regret over that departure as an act of disloyalty to herself.

"But she was like a second mother to me," Arabella remembered telling Serena. "It is only natural that I will miss her."

"I expect you would have preferred that she remain, looking down her long nose at me and whispering to your father that I was not good enough to be his wife," an angry Serena had retorted.

"No, of course that is not what I would have preferred. How can you imagine such a thing, Serena?"

"I do not imagine it," Serena had snapped. "And I hope that I am wrong in believing that you are in agreement with her."

"You are certainly wrong. How many times must I tell you that I am delighted that you are married to Papa, and here, where I have always wanted you to be."

"Is that really the truth?" Serena had demanded.

"Of course it is." Arabella had flung her arms around her. "You know how fond I am of you."

Serena had kissed her then and admitted that she might have been mistaken. She seemingly had dismissed the matter of Arabella's supposed disloyalty from her mind.

However, a short time later, there had been that moment when Arabella had shown Serena through the portrait gallery, recounting bits of amusing gossip about one or another ancestor. She had not immediately realized that Serena imagined that she was speaking out of pride and, in the process, trying to make her feel small because her knowledge of her own family stretched no farther back than her grandfather on her father's side. Serena's mother, though well-born, belonged to a house ennobled in the days of George II. Again, she had been mollified by Arabella's reassurances that she had meant no such thing.

The situation that had arisen after Lord Ashmore commissioned Serena's own portrait was even more unfortunate. Though she had made little of being painted, Arabella guessed that Serena was secretly delighted, especially since the artist selected to paint her was none other than the great Sir Thomas Lawrence.

They had met the artist in the portrait gallery and Sir Thomas had greeted Serena pleasantly, saying that he was surprised and delighted to have so lovely a subject. Then his eye had been drawn to the other portraits, and in examining them, he had noted the strong family resemblance between Arabella and her ancestors. He had then interestedly studied her face, describing how he would paint her. He had gone on to discuss various ways of posing her—much to Serena's annoyance.

An embarrassed Arabella had wanted to bring him back to the subject at hand, but it had been impossible to interrupt him. Oblivious of both young women and intent on the way he wished to present one whom he obviously admired, he had spoken rapidly, his gaze lingering on her face rather than on Serena's. He had appeared rather discomfited when Arabella had gently reminded him that he was to paint Serena.

Serena, of course, had taken his interest in Arabella to mean that he did not believe her aristocratic enough to be included in that distinguished company of noble lords and ladies. Furthermore, she had subsequently taxed Arabella for not reminding him immediately that she was not to be his subject. Again, Arabella had managed to assure her that it would have been difficult to break into that flowing discourse.

Serena had finally agreed that she was right, but unfortunately the argument had taken place in the portrait gallery after Sir Thomas' departure and Arabella's eye had been drawn to a portrait done when her Aunt Olivia had been a young girl. She had gone up to it, thinking that her aunt looked very lovely in the painting, so young and so full of gaiety. Ignoring her comments on the young man who had so cruelly deserted her aunt when her dowry was swallowed up in the bankruptcy that had sent Lord Ashmore to India, Serena had crossly accused her of still mourning Lady Olivia's departure.

"Do not tell me that you do not miss her?" she had said challengingly.

"Of course I miss her, but I am glad you are here in her place," Arabella had assured her with what she believed to be consummate tact.

"In *her* place?" Serena had questioned irately. "I am not in her place. I am your father's wife, not his elderly unmarried sister."

Unwisely, in view of the situation, Arabella had retorted edgily, "My aunt is not elderly, unless you imagine thirty-three to be elderly. Papa, I might remind you, is six years her senior."

"You are saying that your father is elderly?" Serena had demanded furiously. "I do not believe he would agree with you, nor do I."

Arabella recalled that she had been conscious of a strong desire to hit Serena. It had also occurred to her that her friend's reasoning was singularly elliptical— and even daft. However, she had quickly thrust that conclusion out of her mind, reminding herself that Lady Olivia was probably the main bone of contention and that her aunt had never troubled to conceal her dislike for Serena.

Unfortunately, that particular confrontation had had unanticipated ramifications when her father, taking her aside, had asked Arabella what she meant by calling him "old" to his young wife. She had painstakingly explained Serena's error, but she had feared him to be hurt and his hurt, in turn, had hurt her. Furthermore, she was not at all sure that he believed the lengthy explanation she had given him, until an angry Serena had accused her of carrying tales to her father.

That storm had been of short duration, but on pondering it now, Arabella decided that was when the rift had first occurred. Then, shortly after that, Serena had made a new friend, who swiftly became her confidante.

The friend, Lady Frances Villiers, was the recent bride of Sir Humphrey Villiers, who in past years had been Arabella's playmate. Lady Frances was one of the first to call on the bride and they had liked each other immediately.

Serena had subsequently given a tea attended by, among others, Sir Humphrey and Lady Villiers, during which he and Arabella had greeted each other joyfully and proceeded to discuss and laugh over sundry episodes in their childhood. Later, Serena had taxed Arabella for speaking far too familiarly with Sir Humphrey. She had told her that Lady Frances was very sensitive and that it was quite apparent to the lady that Arabella had enjoyed a far closer relationship with her husband than his wife had suspected.

"Than she had suspected?" Arabella had echoed, trying hard to keep her temper and unsuccessfully quelling her sarcasm. "What, pray, might her lady-ship suspect of a friendship that began when we were four and five years of age and ended when we were nine and ten? We played together until he went off to Eton, and the next year I went to school in Bath. Yes, he did write to me while we were at school, and if you will be pleased to recall, Serena, I was in the habit of reading his letters to you. He was far fonder of playing the most horrid practical jokes on me than making love to me, and I pray you will acquaint her foolish ladyship of that fact—if Humphrey has not already done so."

All these minor flurries were, however, nothing to the rage that consumed Serena when her godmother, the elderly Duchess of Mere, sent for Arabella—an invitation that included Lord Ashmore but excluded his recent bride.

In vain, a regretful Lord Ashmore patiently explained that the duchess was eighty-three years old and that she was the great-great-aunt of Arabella's mother and that she had been present at the late Lady Ashmore's christening as well as that of her daughter. Serena, however, refused to be mollified. She insisted that the duchess had purposely overlooked his bride because, probably, she had been in communication with Lady Olivia and had heard horrid, untrue gossip about her brother's marriage and had also learned that she was not of the ancient aristocracy!

In the interests of peace, Arabella had wanted to refuse the invitation, but her father had insisted that she accept what was tantamount to a royal command. They had both gone to the duchess's castle, and her ladyship, gazing vaguely at Arabella out of faded blue eyes, had seemed to mistake her for her grandmother and had talked happily of the time that they had been friends of Sarah Lennox, whom everybody thought would marry the Prince of Wales, dear Georgie. She had spoken as if the prince and Sarah were only in the next room. Then, in a brief fit of lucidity she had given Arabella a diamond bracelet and had nodded her out of the chamber, subsequently falling back into vagueness and saying loudly enough for her departing guests to hear, "Who were those two people and why did they stay so long?"

Arabella had furnished Serena with an amusing and detailed description of that meeting, but though she had appeared to be amused, Arabella had been made aware from various little comments Serena had let drop that she was still deeply wounded by what she insisted in describing as the duchess's "slight."

It was shortly after this episode that Lord Kinnard, having met Serena in the stretch of woods lying between their two estates, was invited to dinner. In a very short time, he had become the good friend of the young woman he had once both detested and denigrated. As for Serena, she pronounced herself extremely impressed by his fine manners, his charm, and by what she was pleased to describe as his deep love for her stepdaughter in spite of the way Arabella had been teasing him. Subsequently, Serena had become his champion and achieved a notable triumph in the field of what she called "love."

" 'And will I then be wed tomorrow morn . . .' " The words of Juliet's soliloquy came back to Arabella's mind. " 'Were I forced to wed him, I would take a dagger to my bed,' " she murmured, staring bleakly out of the window again. She was alone in the house—alone save for the servants, of course. Serena and Lord Ashmore had gone to visit one of his old friends in another county. They would not be back until the end of the week, and as a parting reminder, a triumphant Serena had told her that she had asked the village's best seamstress to send to London for patterns for her wedding gown. The first fitting, she had continued, would take place when they returned—Tuesday week.

She had spoken with such complacency that Arabella had longed to hit her, but she had kept a clenched hand at her side and merely wished her a pleasant journey. She had not given those wishes a warm inflection and she recalled the chill glance she received from her erstwhile friend as she had said, "I had hoped we might dwell together in peace, Arabella. I had not expected to encounter your unreasonable jealousy and your reprehensible efforts to separate your father and me with your cunning lies. I know now that you gave only lip-service to a friendship I once prized most highly. However, my husband is well-acquainted with your schemes and he agrees with me that he never really knew you for what you are.''

By the time that an astonished Arabella had framed a retort to this astonishing statement, Serena had gone. Arabella thought now that it was more than possible that Serena was mad.

Was she?

The mad were known to be cunning, and if they were beautiful as well, they might easily hide their infirmity under a smiling and pleasant exterior. Furthermore, the mad were often known to have a peculiar ability to make the false sound true—and certainly Serena was gifted in that respect. Arabella cast her mind back over their school years. Serena had not seemed mad then, but there had been those times when she had wandered off without explanation, had seemingly been unaware that she had done anything out of the way. There had also been her failure to write. Perhaps her experiences upon leaving school, coupled with her misery over her father's changed circumstances and subsequent incarceration in the Fleet Prison for debt, had had a deleterious effect on her mind. Yet, whatever the reason for Serena's peculiar behavior and the strong dislike in which she seemed to hold her, Arabella realized she could not remain at home. She grimaced, thinking of the drastic step she was about to take. Certainly, it filled her with trepidation, but she had no other recourse. Were she to remain under her father's roof, she must marry a man she loathed!

''No,'' she breathed, and in her mind's eye she saw once again that playbill which might prove her salvation. It had announced the arrival of the Gordon Company in Lincoln, a city fortunately not far from the hold. They would be at the Theatre Royal for a fortnight and she would be leaving for Lincoln this afternoon!

She would take the gig, which she could drive herself, and Lizzie would accompany her. Her abigail was only two years her senior, but she had a purposeful air and could fill the role of chaperon. She would tell the servants that she was visiting an old friend who lived nearby. Quite a few of the staff had transferred loyalty to Serena, but not Lizzie nor the stable boys who had promised to harness the gig. She would take a bandbox with her, concealed under her cloak, and once at the theater, she would beg Julian Sherlay to get her to London and to her aunt. She would have to borrow the money from him, having only a few odd coins in pin money. She hoped he would help her, if only out of his great anger and disappoint over Serena's cruelty.

She could not hope for more, given his treatment, and it was possible that he might not want to see her because of her inadvertent connection with the situation. Yet, he could hardly blame her for what had taken place, and he might even sympathize with her. She rose and some few minutes later she rang for Lizzie.

As she had hoped, Arabella's departure from her home was managed with amazing ease. She had had the cooperation of all the stable boys and those footmen who had not gone with Lord Ashmore and his lady. They had told the housekeeper that Lady Arabella would need the post chaise this afternoon, the gig having broken down. Arabella had specified a meeting with the mantua maker to describe the bride clothes she planned to have made.

"You'll 'ave to take the post chaise," Mark had

insisted. "You shouldn't be seen in yon gig, milady. Might run into a brace o' gawkers, 'n even though ye'll be wearin' a veil over yer bonnet, there's no tellin' what a breeze might do. We'll drive, 'n ye'll 'ave plenty o' protection."

"But if I do not come back, you might be in grave trouble with my father," she had pointed out.

"Us'll 'ave a tale for that, milady, never fear."

They had reached Lincoln at a little past the hour of one in the afternoon. Lizzie, inquiring backstage at the Theatre Royal, had been told that the actors were rehearsing, and now Arabella, waiting in the greenroom, moved back and forth across the chamber. The custodian had delivered her message to Julian. Would he come during a break? Or would he hold her in anathema as the stepdaughter of the woman he had loved?

She smoothed out the smile that came to her lips. It was mirthless, to be sure, but she must not be smiling, not even at the great joke that had brought her here, a fugitive from a household ruled by the young woman who had once been her best friend—and whom she had so happily, so proudly, introduced to her father.

Serena was not much of a reader, but certainly she must have read "Cinderella" and conned the role of the wicked stepmother. Waves of anger coursed through her mind as she thought of Serena's machinations. Arabella was now suddenly positive that the reason she had never heard from Serena until that fateful meeting in Brighton sprang from the latter's jealousy. Now that she thought of it, Camilla had once told her that Serena had a jealous nature. They had argued about it until Camilla had reluctantly conceded that she might be wrong.

However, she had not been wrong. Serena was not only jealous, she was also a notable actress, for she had disguised her true nature and, off stage, she had turned in a most remarkable performance—one worthy of a Sarah Siddons, indeed.

She had managed to estrange her dearest friend from her father with very little difficulty because, as Serena was well aware, Arabella herself had been just getting to know him. She had told a great many lies very convincingly. Of course, she had been unconsciously aided by Lady Olivia, who might have been a buffer between Serena and her brother, but who, well aware of the bride's true nature, had left. Then, Serena, wishing to be alone with her husband, had determined that she would be, and had accomplished her purpose with no loose ends—or so she had believed.

She had not, however, counted on her protected friend seizing the reins of her destiny in her own two hands. Serena had ridden off in triumph, but she would return, hopefully, to defeat, at least in one facet of her careful plans for the future.

"Lady Arabella!"

Arabella looked up and there was Mr. Sherlay standing in the doorway leading from the stage. He closed the door behind him and moved toward her while she stared at him apprehensively, her heart pounding. The fear that he would not welcome her was larger in her mind now. He was thinner and he looked older . . . No, not really older, she amended, but so very unhappy.

"Mr. Sherlay," she began as she, too, rose. Then, though she had meant to speak to him in a cool, dignified manner, to state her problem succinctly, to ask if he might take her to London or, failing that, advance her the monies for the stagecoach fare, all she could say was, "Oh, sir, I beg you will help me. I am in such utter despair." Tears filled her eyes and, overflowing, ran down her cheeks.

"Oh, milady, do not . . ." Lizzie was at her side. She looked anxiously up at the actor. "Oh, sir, please 'elp 'er."

He looked confused as he regarded the two unhappy young women. "I will be glad to help you in whatever way I may," he assured them quickly. "At present, however, I am still in rehearsal. You must both come into the theater. When we are finished, I will take you to a place where we can be private."

The auditorium was dark, damp, and cavernous, lighted only by the candles that stood on a table downstage left and by the flickering glow from two or three footlights. However, Mr. Sherlay made his way quickly enough to a pair of seats on the aisle, and breathing a caution to be quiet, he hurried up the four steps to the stage.

The company was rehearsing *The Beggar's Opera*, said to be a great favorite with audiences in that particular town. Mrs. Gordon was, of course, Polly and Mr. Gordon played old Peachum, her father. Mrs. Eddington was her mother, and Nora Paine, one of the younger members of the company, played Lucy Lockit. Mr. Sherlay, of course, played Captain MacHeath, the highwayman.

Arabella was both pleased and surprised to hear him sing his song in a full, rich baritone voice. He spoke his lines with gusto and his actions with Polly were both funny and lewd. Yet, whenever he stood in the wings, his face, in repose, was somber and there was an air of settled unhappiness about him that had certainly not been in evidence when last she had seen him, and that less than three months ago! Obviously, poor Mr. Sherlay had been badly hurt by Serena's defection, and Arabella feared that, given his sensitive nature and his passion for her erstwhile friend, he might not recover soon. Wryly, she remembered her aunt's stories of Lord Ashmore's grief for his young wife's early demise. It had taken him close on twenty years to recover from the shock. Would Mr. Sherlay be similarly afflicted over a woman who did not merit the squandering of a single one of his thoughts?

"Ooooh, just listen to him, One'd think 'e were a real 'ighwayman," Lizzie murmured.

"Yes, he's a fine actor," Arabella whispered, thinking that there was no one in London who could match him and, at the same time, feeling happier because she was here in surroundings she loved and watching Mr. Sherlay perform. She had a sudden wish that she might remain with the company, but that, of course, was not possible. And in the midst of these thoughts, suddenly Mr. Sherlay was beside her, nearly faceless in that dim light.

"Come, Lady Arabella," he said gently, "I have nowhere to bring you save the King's Head, where I will bespeak a private room, if you have no objection."

"No, I have not, Mr. Sherlay," she assured him hastily.

"Come, then," he said. "Your girl will go with you."

Much to Arabella's surprise, none of the people in the tavern that lay cheek-by-jowl with the Theatre Royal paid any attention to a veiled lady and her rather nervous little abigail as they proceeded Mr.

Sherlay into a small paneled room furnished with a rough oak table and four chairs.

Bidding them sit down, he ordered wine and tea and waited until it was served before turning to Arabella, his eyes wide with concern as he asked, "Pray, what is amiss, my dear Lady Arabella?"

She began hesitantly, not knowing whether or not she ought to disillusion him about Serena, but once she had mentioned her name, it seemed that the words flowed from her lips almost without volition. Passionately, angrily, and with a strong feeling of pain as well as betrayal, she recounted the strange change that had come over one whom she had believed to be her dearest friend.

He listened in a surprised and, ultimately, a frowning silence. Then, as she brought her explanation to a close, he said slowly, "They are determined that you marry this man?"

"Yes," she said unhappily. "Serena has managed to convince my father that I confessed my love for him to her, and there is no making him believe otherwise, else he would have to think her a liar. It is far easier for him to put that onus on me, and he will not listen to any further argument. I cannot imagine what Serena has told him, but that does not matter. I cannot, I will not marry him. I hate him."

"No, of course you cannot marry him. I remember him . . . a very unpleasant young man," Mr. Sherlay said with an edge of anger to his own voice.

"Oh, yes, he is. I am so glad you agree," she sighed. "I must go to London, to my aunt. Do you suppose that you might . . ." She hesitated and then added reluctantly, "I have no money. Could you lend me the money for the stage coach. You have but to give me the direction of the company in the next few weeks and I will send it back to you." Before he could reply, she added hastily, "I expect you must wonder why I am appealing to you? There is none other I could ask. Most of the people I know live miles from us, and there is Sir Humphrey, but Serena has become good friends with his wife, and were I to call upon him—"

"I beg you will say no more," he said quickly. "I quite understand your situation, but, my dear Lady Arabella, you cannot go by the stage."

"I will have Lizzie with me."

"Aye, that she will," the abigail said staunchly.

"And neither of you strong enough to contend with the rogues that travel the stage. It is out of the question, Lady Arabella," he said firmly.

She stood up, gazing up at him defiantly. "I must go to London, sir. I will not go back if that is what you are suggesting."

He had been looking sober and even somber, but now a smile played about his mouth and gleamed in his eyes. "I beg you will sit down, Lady Arabella. I was not suggesting that you go back. Indeed, it is unthinkable! Your place is with your aunt."

"But . . . how?" she began confusedly.

"Heed me. In a matter of three weeks, I will be going to London. I will be pleased to escort you and your abigail, if you do not mind waiting."

A glimmer of hope flickered in her mind, but she said nervously, "I have no place to stay and no funds."

"I will see that you find a place. Mrs. Gordon and her husband will be pleased to help you." He frowned. "I hope you did not arrive on the stage."

"No," she explained about the stable hands.

"Very good . . ." He stared thoughtfully at her.

"Undoubtedly there will be people looking for you. There might even be a hue and cry. I think that for the next three weeks, you will need to be kept out of sight as much as possible. You could remain backstage."

"I could prompt," she said quickly. "I could relieve whoever is on the book. In the daytime, I could help out in other ways. I can sew and I would be glad to work on the costumes if such work is needed. I know a little about theater from school."

He looked dubious, then he said slowly, "But why not? They would not look for you among the costumes or peering into the prompt book or even walking across the stage as a painted super-numerary . . ."

"Oh," she breathed. "I would like *that* above all things."

He gave her a warm smile. "Very well, little . . . Sarah, we will chance it."

"Oh, Mr. Sherlay," she whispered. "Oh, I do thank you . . . but Sarah?"

"I will have to call you Sarah or Meg or anything save your real name. Tell me which you favor?"

"Derwent," she supplied, using the name of her most favorite governess.

"Sarah Derwent," he said musingly. "Yes, I like it." He nodded.

"And so do I," she said gratefully. Other words trembled on her lips, but she did not voice them, did not tell him that she longed to match this new name with a new life, a life in the theater—a long life in the theater with him.

7

The auditorium was reasonably quiet, even though on occasion there were loud laughs from the gallery and annoyed requests for silence from the pit. There was also the usual rustling of playbills and there were sighs, coughs, giggles, sneezes, as well as loud conversations carried on between various members of the audience and some bawdy remarks directed to the actresses on stage—all the sounds to which Arabella, now in her second week as prompter, was becoming happily accustomed as she sat backstage. Her gaze was on the prompt book for *School for Scandal*, with its scribbles, its dog-eared pages, these needing to be lifted carefully so they would not rattle as she peered at the lines and, on occasion, spoke them for the benefit of that extremely indifferent actress Eloise Bradley, who played Maria.

Actually, until this morning, Eloise had been the understudy for Imogen Maltravers, who suddenly and without warning had left the company the previous night. Poor Eloise, who usually played maids or a member of a crowd or a mere walk-on, had been chosen to stand by because she was pert, pretty, and not afraid of an audience. However, she had obviously not learned the role and she was faltering badly, badly enough to warrant catcalls from the balcony and disparaging remarks from the pit.

Arabella winced as a man suddenly yelled, "What 'ave we 'ere? A milkmaid or an abigail? Sure she's no actress."

"Tha's wot I say . . . Take 'er off, take 'er off," someone cried from the balcony. "Take 'er off, take 'er off . . ." Several other people joined in.

Of a sudden, the theater was filled with murmurs and loud chatter as some members of the audience loudly denigrated the complainers while others, equally loud, voiced a veritable chorus of disagreement. There was also the loud drumming of feet on the hardwood floor.

"Damn," muttered Julian, who was standing a short distance from Arabella and looking magnificent in his powdered wig and satin coat. "The chit has the presence of a mouse."

" 'Tis only the first act," someone screamed. "Shall we bear with this nothing until the play's end?"

"No, I say, no," another man cried.

"Nooooooo . . ." chorused some boys.

"Noooo, take 'er off," echoed other members of the audience, together with more drumming of feet.

Fortunately, they were near the end of the first scene and mercifully the curtains closed.

Eloise, dashing off the stage, began to sob loudly in the wings. "I want to go home," she wailed.

"My dear." A harried Mrs. Gordon in Lady Teazle's garb put a comforting arm around her shaking shoulders. "My dear, you cannot leave . . . there's no replacement."

"I do not care! I will not go out there again," Eloise moaned.

"Come, child," rasped Mr. Gordon, who was

fighting against a rising anger. "You've little more to say."

"I will not go out on that stage again." Eloise glared at him. "I hate being an actress. It's horrid."

"Eloise, my dear," Julian said gently, "you are just frightened. Once you calm down—"

"No, no, no, I want to go hommmmmmme," she wailed.

"If you please." Arabella had moved to Eloise's side. "I know the role, and we are much of a size. Might I not go on in her place?"

"No," Julian said firmly. "You cannot!"

"Why not?" Mr. Gordon demanded. "Why not, indeed?"

"But, sir, you know what she is and—"

"The audience don't know," Mrs. Gordon murmured. She bent an eye on Arabella. "Do you think you can do it, my dear?"

Arabella said firmly, "I know I can. And Lizzie, my abigail, can read—she can stay on the book."

"There," exclaimed the erstwhile Maria. "You have her and she can fit into my costumes."

"Come, come." Mr. Gordon touched his wife's arm. "It's our scene, Lady Teazle."

"Yes, Sir Peter," she murmured, and casting a glance over her shoulder, she added hastily, "You'll not be needed until Act Two, Scene Two, but you'd best hurry and look over your lines, my dear."

"I know them," Arabella whispered. "I know the whole play."

"I still do not think . . ." Julian frowned.

"We have no choice, dear boy," Mr. Gordon said firmly, and led his wife toward the stage.

"She will have three more scenes to go," Mrs. Eddington muttered.

"Exactly." Julian nodded.

"And I will have to perform with her," Mr. Amory, the young man playing the part of Joseph Surface, darted a nervous glance at Arabella.

"I had best get changed," she said firmly.

"I expect we will have to take the chance," Julian said reluctantly. "Otherwise, we will be in shambles. They're prepared to destroy Maria the next time she appears." He turned to Arabella, adding worriedly, "You are aware of that, are you not?"

She said softly, "I am not afraid, Julian."

"Good girl," he said surprisingly. "Break a leg, then."

She did not misunderstand him. "I will do my best, sir."

"Come and change," Eloise said crossly. "I wish to be out of here."

"Aye, and good riddance," muttered Mr. Amory. "I was expecting to be hit with an old shoe or a rotten apple."

"And 'twould serve you right." Eloise stuck her tongue out at the actor.

"Go along with you," Mrs. Eddington hissed. "The child must have time to get into character."

"Come, come, that is asking too much." Mr. Amory raised thin eyebrows.

"Be silent." Julian glared at him. He turned to Arabella, "Hurry, my dear. You'll need to do lines with Amory here."

"Yes," she said breathlessly, and followed Eloise into the dressing room.

In an amazingly short time Arabella, clad in Maria's

costume, was standing in the wings with Mrs. Gordon, who was, as usual, clad in Lady Teazle's exaggerated gown with its immense paniers and wide skirts. She was also wearing a towering powdered wig. Maria's costume, though simpler, also needed managing when it came to the paniers. Fortunately, her wig was rather understated and fitted closely to the head. However, as she waited there, she wondered how it had come to pass that she was there at all?

Mentally, she wished herself a thousand miles away—a million miles—and meanwhile, in her head was a veritable jumble of the lines she had read in the prompter's book during three different performances. And which was she to utter first? And when? And who would give her the cue? She shivered and received a quick look from Mrs. Gordon and a warm clasp of her hand together with a smile and a nod. Then, suddenly she moved forward, and Arabella, thinking of nothing at all, went with her onto that bright stage, a stage fronted by an equally brightly lighted house, lamps under all the boxes and flaming candles in a huge chandelier, dripping with rainbow-hued crystal. A glance at the auditorium showed her a veritable ocean of faces, and with a little gasp, she glanced down quickly.

As the actors had anticipated, there were catcalls and whistles from all areas of the theater. There were also loud, raucous, and, on occasion, rude and even obscene commands for Maria to remove herself and enter some other line of work, this despite the fact that Mr. Gordon had announced the change in cast. However, Mrs. Blackwell as Mrs. Candour spoke her first line calmly enough. ''I must have a copy,'' she said while Mrs. Eddington as Lady Sneerwell, fixed her eyes on Mrs. Gordon, saying, " 'Lady Teazle, I hope we will see Sir Peter?' "

Then, Mrs. Gordon was replying, " 'I am sure he will wait on your ladyship, presently.' "

Mrs. Eddington, turning her chill gaze on Arabella, said, " 'Maria, my love, you look grave. Come, you shall sit down to piquet with Mr. Surface.' "

They were all looking at her and there were more titters, more guffaws, more catcalls, and more jeers from the audience.

Arabella guessed that the spectators were primed to loathe her, but Maria's lines forced themselves into her benumbed consciousness, and assuming a grave, judicious look, she said clearly, " 'I take very little pleasure in cards—however, I'll do as your ladyship pleases.' "

Then she sat down across the small card table from Mr. Amory as Joseph Surface or, rather, she was across the table from *Joseph Surface*, aware of his admiring gaze as he laid out the cards; and, totally in the character of Maria, she wished strongly that his brother Charles were facing her from Joseph's chair.

The play was finally at an end and the applause was loud and sustained. Arabella, bowing dazedly beside Julian, was not sure what she felt until later—much later, when the actors crowded around her warmly congratulating her on her poise, her line reading, and her overall excellence. Confusedly, she heard herself telling Mr. Gordon that she would learn the role of Lucy Lockit and understudy Juliet, assignments that had been the portion of Eloise Bradley. She would, she said, do it until they could get a proper replacement. She did not add that she hoped they would never find such a replacement, and she had a strong feeling that the Gordons intended to let her remain with the company, something she confided to Lizzie once she was back in her lodgings.

"Oh, milady!" The abigail looked distressed. "I do not know, I am sure."

"What do you not know, Lizzie?" Arabella asked as she prepared to crawl into the hard little bed in the tiny room at the King's Head Inn.

"Supposin' yer father was to find out?"

"How could he find me out? I am known as Sarah Derwent," Arabella said.

" 'E'll be lookin' for you . . . sendin' out the Runners, maybe."

"I doubt it," Arabella said coldly. "He is far too happy with his bride to waste any time wondering what might have happened to his daughter. No, I am quite safe here, Lizzie, but if you would prefer to return, I will certainly understand."

"Oh, no, I would never leave you, milady," the girl insisted almost tearfully. "May I be nibbled on by ducks if I would."

Though she was hardly in the mood for laughter, Arabella could not restrain a giggle. "I should not like to see you meet so horrid a fate, Lizzie; consequently I am delighted by your decision. Now, if you please, let us both retire for the night. It has been a very long day."

"Yes, milady," Lizzie said, but her look as she blew out the candles clearly suggested that she was still of the opinion that no good would ever come of her mistress's mad venture.

"I do not care what she thinks. I do not care what anybody thinks, I am happy, happy, happy," Arabella whispered to herself, and realized wonderingly that happiness of this particular nature was a relatively new sensation. The only time she had ever experienced anything corresponding to the exhilaration she was currently feeling had taken place when she was performing in the little scenes at school. No, that was not entirely true—there was another far more cogent reason for her happiness and his name was Julian Sherlay.

The company had moved northward to the city of York, and on a chill day in late February, Arabella flanked by the Gordons was standing in the greenroom of the city's Theatre Royal, arguing with a concerned and frowning Julian Sherlay.

"But I know the role of Lucy Lockit through and through, and since Mary is feeling poorly and is hardly in any condition to perform this evening, I do not see why I may not appear. I stood in for Mary at rehearsal today, if you will remember, Julian, and I will not go up in my lines."

"Of course, she will not," Mr. Gordon added his voice to the altercation. "I do not understand you, Julian."

"And nor do I, my dear," Mrs. Gordon looked quizzically at Julian. "You have seen her in several rehearsals of the role. She gives promise of being one of our best Lucys."

"I will certainly not deny that. She does the role very well—too well." He frowned.

"Too well?" Arabella regarded him confusedly. "Then, why?"

"Well, then, if you do it, you must not come to the greenroom after the play, else we will have trouble. We have already had trouble and you were not playing Lucy," he said firmly.

"That trouble was dealt with quickly enough," Mr. Gordon said.

"And nearly had the sheriff down on us for roughing up two members of the audience," Julian reminded him.

"Other members of the audience spoke for us," Mr. Gordon said, but he frowned. "Still it were better, I think, if you remained in the dressing room until Julian can escort you home. Should you mind that, my dear?"

"No, not in the least," Arabella assured him quickly.

"Well, then, that's all right and tight," Mr. Gordon said approvingly.

"Indeed, yes, we do thank you for the suggestion, Julian, dear." Mrs. Gordon smiled warmly at him.

Arabella, however, stifled a sigh. Despite her hasty acquiescence, she found herself disappointed. The role of Lucy Lockit was by far the largest and most important role she had been given, and in her brief time as an actress, she had found herself enjoying the praise she received whenever she enacted the role of Maria.

Occasionally, of course, she had been repelled by some of the rude comments and the looks that had accompanied them, generally addressed to her by the so-called gentlemen who thronged the greenroom, but Julian had always found his way to her side, firmly establishing himself as her protector. But now, she wondered unhappily, was he wearying of that task? Was he beginning to find her constant presence a burden?

He had not protested when she decided to remain with the company, the Gordons having auditioned several aspiring young actresses none of whom, they

declared, pleased them as much as herself. Had he
been secretly disappointed by their decision? It was
hard to guess what he might be thinking. Despite the
fact that she was with him during rehearsals nearly
every day, and despite the fact that he insisted on
taking her to and from the theater, there was none of
the closeness between them that she knew he had
enjoyed with Serena.

Did he, in some strange way, blame her for the loss
of the woman he had loved—might yet love? Did he
see her as her father's daughter rather than a person
in her own right?

She looked toward him and failed to catch his gaze.
He was speaking to Jeremy Stevens, who would be
enacting the role of the Turnkey tonight. She also
noted Miss Carey, who now played Mrs. Peachum,
smiling provocatively up at Julian. Miss Carey was
easily ten years his senior, but that had never
prevented that lusty lady from casting a roguish eye
in his direction. There were others outside the
company who followed her example, females whose
habit it was to take a prominent box and proceed to
ogle the male members of the audience. Invariably,
these lost out to Julian when the fair cyprians turned
their quizzing glasses from pit to stage. And, of
course, there were the ladies of fashion who did not
hesitate to court him. Some sent him costly presents,
and every day scented letters arrived at the theater
with his name scrawled across the envelopes.

Julian, however, was impervious to this attention.
Still, the fact that he sent back the presents and
destroyed the letters did not cheer her. She did not
count these ladies as her rivals: her rival was far away
and her name was Serena.

Anger ran through Arabella as she thought of

Serena's cruel rejection of Julian's love. She alone was responsible for his lingering unhappiness, and each time Arabella glimpsed that somber look in his eyes, she was racked by fury, hating Serena quite as much as she had once adored her. Yet, oddly enough, it was only at such times that she actually thought of her so-called stepmother, and then only in context of the misery she had brought to poor Julian.

As for herself, Serena's machinations had inadvertently enriched her life. These last few months had been the happiest she had ever spent. The constant traveling over bumpy roads in ill-sprung vehicles, the indifferent hostelries with their tiny rooms, their lumpy beds, and their impudent chambermaids who held actresses in contempt, failed to disturb her. Nor did she resent the weariness that came over her after a day's rehearsing and a night's performing. No, she loved it all, because a dream had become reality: she was in the theater, acting in the theater, and hearing the applause of audiences excited and thrilled by her ability at bringing a character to life.

An arm sliding around her waist caused her to tense and to look up angrily, ready to reprimand one or another of the importunate young actors who often tried to flirt with her. However, her anger faded swiftly when she found that the arm belonged to Julian, who said, "Shall we walk to the York Minster. I always try to visit this cathedral when we are in town."

"Oh." She looked up at him, her eyes glowing. "I would love that above all things."

"Above all things." He smiled warmly at her. 'How easily you are pleased, milady.''

"How can I not be pleased in such pleasant

company," she murmured, and was immediately regretful, fearing that she had sounded far too bold.

However, he merely continued to smile. "Your company is pleasant for me, too, my Sarah."

Meeting his eyes, she wondered if she were wrong in thinking that there was a subtle change in his manner—that, of a sudden, a barrier between them had given way? She said softly, "Is it, Julian?"

He regarded her gravely. "I always say what I mean, but I wonder . . . do you?"

She tensed. "Have I ever given you reason to imagine that I do not?"

"You seem honest enough, my dear. Indeed, I am not inpugning that honesty. Still, I cannot help but wonder if you are not confounded by this radical change in your position? Do you really enjoy being with us as much as you insist? You come from wealth and—"

She held up her hand. "Julian, I come from wealth and misery. If I had not been able to get away . . ." She shuddered. "I have told you what happened."

"Yes." He frowned. "You have told me." He shook his head and looked at her wonderingly. "You and Lord Kinnard. Good God, it would seem to me that your father must have seen how very unsuited you are."

She said slowly, "I expect he might have listened to my arguments had not Serena told him I was merely teasing his lordship, and that in my heart of hearts I really cared for him but was not ready to marry as yet. That was the gist of her argument—at least as I understand it from my father."

"She can be very devious," he said regretfully. "She led me to believe . . ." He sighed and shook his head. "But your father, my dear, I do not understand him. Why was *he* so ready to credit her lies? He knew you . . . knows you.''

''No.'' She shook her head. ''He does not know me well enough to doubt her. He was in India most of my life. He did not come home often, and certainly he did not see me at school every day for years as Serena did. She had my entire confidence in those days and I imagine that she convinced him that she had it still.''

He was silent a moment. Then he said slowly, ''Yes, on occasion she can be very convincing.''

She said softly, ''I am sorry, Julian.''

''Do not be,'' he said quickly. The bitterness that had been so apparent before had disappeared, to be replaced by a warm and even affectionate smile. ''Let us take our walk to the minster, and mind you, hold your cloak tight about you. The winds are chill.''

''I will, thank you, sir.'' She met his smile with one of her own.

''If the winds were not so chill, I would suggest we walk around the walls as well,'' he said.

''It is a pity that they are,'' she commented. ''I would enjoy such a walk.'' She was glad he did not know that she would have enjoyed a walk through a snowstorm were he with her. ''You seem very familiar with York.''

''Yes, I am. I used to come here as a lad. My father had friends who lived outside the city. I wish I might also show you Whitby Abbey, which lies close to the sea, but it is far too cold for such an excursion. We might go there some other time, perhaps.''

''Some other time, yes.'' She nodded, feeling her heart throb because he had referred so casually to another time—as if he expected to know her in some distant future—but as soon as that thought crossed her mind, she assured herself that it had been no more than a casual remark meaning nothing.

"The streets are very narrow," he commented a few minutes later. "I had forgotten that."

"Oh, they are," she agreed. "And the houses look as if they were bending toward us. They must be very old."

"Yes, I should say that most of them were built four hundred years ago . . ."

"So old?" she marveled, and then shivered as a blast of cold wind struck her.

"You are cold?" he asked solicitously.

"No, not really."

He put his arm around her, drawing her closer to him. "I think you are. It is very cold this afternoon. Perhaps we'd best go back to the inn."

"Oh, please, not yet," she said quickly, loving the feel of his arm about her shoulders. Then, aware that her hasty response might have sounded too bold, too eager, she added reluctantly, "But you probably have much to do before the performance."

He shook his head. "Later I will need to rest, of course, but if you want to see the minster and are not too cold—"

"I am not," she interrupted, hoping that he would not take his arm away. Much to her relief, he did not. In fact, he drew her a little closer to his side.

In a few minutes they had reached the main entrance of the vast cathedral and stood staring up at its ornate facade flanked by two tall towers constructed, Julian told her, in the late perpendicular period.

"That would be 1375 to 1540," she said glibly, and then flushed as he smiled at her saying, "Yes, those are the dates and you learned them in school, as did

I. And listened to my teacher mourn the passing of the so-called decorated period, circa 1275 to 1375.''

"The most perfect style that English architecture ever attained,'' she said.

He laughed. "Ah, we have both been taught by pedagogues who were deeply in love with the glorious past, which always seems so much more beguiling than the mundane present.''

"I would not agree with that,'' she said.

He came to a stop. "Would you not?''

She gazed up into his face, his startlingly handsome face, strong-featured and lighted by his large dark eyes. Behind him rose the mighty cathedral and she had the odd fancy that the man before her seemed to belong to both the past and the present. He could have been a knight-at-arms bound toward the cathedral to seek a blessing for some adventure or, more likely, quest. In that moment she knew that she loved him with all her heart, but she thought yearningly, that sensation was not new. She had been experiencing it ever since she had locked glances with him all those months ago.

How long had she loved him?

She was not precisely sure. She only knew that he had, and with consummate ease, drawn her heart from her bosom. Unfortunately, he did not want it and would never know that it belonged to him.

8

A strong, cold March wind carrying with it a remainder of February's frost was howling around the theater on the night marking the Gordon players' final performance in York.

On the afternoon of the next day, the company would be traveling to Richmond, where their first offering would be taking place on Friday of the following week. Arabella, huddled in her cloak, shivered as she listened to the plaint of the wind. She could also feel it, for the dressing room was old and there were cracks in the windowpanes. Indeed, she was wishing strongly that she might have played prim Maria rather than lusty Lucy. She joined the other actors in the greenroom; she was, she thought resentfully, growing colder by the minute.

Mrs. Gordon and Mrs. Eddington had remarked on the chill and hurried into their clothes as fast as they could change. The other women were of a similar opinion but all of them enjoined her to wait until Julian could leave the greenroom and come to fetch her.

" 'Tis a rough crowd tonight, my love." Mrs. Gordon had shaken her head. "And you were a most convincing Lucy. But I need not tell you that—you heard the reaction in the audience when you took your curtain calls, and from the men especially! Such a stamping of feet, I never did hear. And there was some I thought were going to come right up on the stage after you.''

Thinking about her words, Arabella was both pleased and regretful. She was glad to have done well, and indeed, she was perfectly aware that she had made the part her own. However, she had caught the older woman's hint that to do well as Lucy Lockit was to enact the part of a whore with a fidelity that might spell trouble were she to meet any of the male members of the audience.

Many of these had not hesitated to express their approval of Mistress Lucy and Mistress Polly, too, in terms that had made Julian furious. He had directed many a surreptitious look at her while they were acting together, and she feared that he would be protesting against her playing such a role again. However, she doubted that the Gordons would heed him. They, too, had lavished considerable praise upon Lucy, and so had his best friend, Byron Capell, who was playing Lockit, the jailer. Some of the women in the cast were not so enthusiastic, but that did not matter as long as the Gordons were in her corner. Neither, she thought amusedly, was willing to credit Julian with her discovery, for all they were so fond of him.

A sigh shook her. She wished that she could be merely fond of Julian, a feeling he undoubtedly had for her. Unfortunately, fondness was far too small a word to express all she felt for him, not even the word "love" was quite adequate. In addition to these feelings, there was need—a need that had made her understand the character of Lucy Lockit very well—Lucy and Polly and even innocent little Juliet! Every day, every moment she was with Julian, she became prey to all the disquieting physical symptoms that spelled need. Her heart pounded, her breath seemed to desert her, and various pulses made themselves known. She was experiencing them now, and suddenly despite the chill in the dressing room, she felt uncomfortably warm and deeply in need of a breath of air. If Lizzie were with her, she might have ventured outside . . . Indeed, where had her abigail gone after she helped her out of her costume and into her gown?

Of late, she had developed a habit of slipping away without saying where she was going. It was possible that she was talking to Jem, who drove Mrs. Eddington's coach. She had a particular liking for him, and Jem, a tall, husky young man, appeared equally interested in Lizzie, fortunate Lizzie, who had found a relationship free from complications! Probably Jem was still here waiting for Mrs. Eddington. There were coaches lined up along the street not too far away, and she had a very good idea that she would find Lizzie there. The presence of her abigail would afford her the protection she needed—yes, even in the greenroom. With Lizzie in tow, she would be protected.

Rising, she hurried to the door opening on the small plot of land back of the theater. As she came out, she saw that there were several vehicles still lined up on the street, among them a post chaise with an elaborate gold monogram on the door, belonging to one or another of the nobles who frequented the theater. She grimaced. Some of them were very obnoxious. They talked loudly while the actors were speaking, and made lewd remarks to the actresses while they surveyed them through their quizzing glasses. On this very night, two young men had turned their glasses on her and had also said things she would as lief not remember. Fortunately a man beside them had quieted them in no uncertain terms.

She grimaced. One met with such ruffians in every theater across the land. Mrs. Gordon had told her some horrendous tales about some of the unfortunate young actresses who had fallen prey to these amorous rakes. She had not to dwell on them now, she reminded herself. She must search for Lizzie. Though it was dark, there was enough light from the coach lanterns to see her abigail unless, naughty child, she had climbed into his equipage with Jem.

"And who have we here?" An insinuating masculine voice brought Arabella out of her thoughts.

"By God, Bruce, it's the little Lockit," commented another, equally insinuating voice.

Startled, Arabella looked up to find two young men standing before her—one was dark and the other fair. Both were dressed in the height of fashion and both were grinning at her. She did not like their grins, and even less did she like the look in their eyes, also illuminated by the coach lanterns. In another second, she had recognized them and with a sinking heart knew them for the pair who had spoken to her in the theater. She cast a hasty look over her shoulder at the door behind her and was distressed to find it farther away than she had anticipated. Still, turning back, she started toward it, only to have the man addressed as Bruce stride after her and put a heavy hand on her shoulder.

"Not so fast, my lovely," he said softly. "We was looking for you in the greenroom, wasn't we, Nick?"

"Aye." The fair-haired young man now stood on

Arabella's other side. "I thought that all actresses came to the greenroom."

"And so they ought," Bruce said. "You should have come there, little Lucy. We was looking for you." His hand pressed down on her shoulder.

She glared up at him. "I will thank you to remove your hand, sir," she said icily.

He did not remove his hand. He only increased the pressure. "But I have no such intention, my beautiful." He peered at her. "You are beautiful, a sight more beautiful without all that garish paint on your face—and lips that want kissing." To her horror, he bent forward and kissed her, a horrid, invading kiss such as she had never experienced before. She coughed and struggled in his tight embrace, but her efforts were futile. He held her fast while he pressed yet another long kiss on her mouth.

"Let me go . . . let me gooooo," she screamed as soon as she could speak. "You've no right, damn you! Let me go."

"Aye, let her go, Bruce. 'Tis my turn now. Share and share alike, I say." Laughing loudly, his friend pushed Bruce aside, and wrapping his arms around Arabella, he gave her a similar and even longer kiss. "I vow," he said as he raised his head. "This lass'll furnish us some rare sport."

"Damn you," she screamed, pounding on his chest with both fists. "Let me go, let me go."

Reaching out a large hand, he caught both of her slender wrists in one hand, clutching them tightly, hurtfully, as he said in laughter-punctuated speech, "We'll be letting you go, lass, in due time . . . come morning or maybe a couple of mornings hence, if you continue to provide us with enough enjoyment. Of course, like all little fillies, you need a bit of gentling.''

"And shall have it," the man he had addressed as Bruce said. "Let's get her to the curricle and be off."

"Noooo, nooo." She struggled futilely against her captor, who was inexorably dragging her toward the line of coaches.

"Come, come, my little tiger-kitten, you'll not be the loser." Her captor grinned. "You are an entertainer, are you not? Well, we crave entertainment and we'll pay you whatever you are worth. Fifty pounds. How does that sound to you, my lovely little whore?"

" 'Ere, wot are you about?"

A struggling, sobbing Arabella heard Jem's familiar voice. "Jem, help me, help me," she cried.

"Aye, lass." He began to move forward, but at that moment a shot rang out.

"Stand back you," ordered one of Arabella's captors. "Unless you'd like a ball through your damned thick head."

"Let me go," Arabella screamed again.

"Aye, in due time, little Lucy, in due time . . ." Picking her up and unmindful of her furious struggles, Nick bore her toward a waiting curricle. "Bruce," he called. "open the door and help me put this prize inside."

"Aye," a piping voice responded as a small tiger came forward.

"Let me go," she screamed futilely as the tiger obediently opened the door of the curricle.

"Lord, it's a veritable lioness," her captor said breathlessly, "and should promise rare sport."

She continued to struggle. "Let me go!"

"In due time, my lovely." Her captor laughed, "Tomorrow, or tomorrow week, depending on—"

"You will let her go now, damn you both to hell," said an irate voice.

Nick stiffened. He did not release Arabella, but on turning, his laughter rang out. "By God, I believe it's the bold Captain MacHeath. Are you the whoremaster off stage, too? How much will you take for this prime bit o' muslin? Oof!" His hold on Arabella loosening, he staggered back, a hand to his assaulted bleeding mouth.

"You damned rogue!" His companion advanced on Julian, who in that same moment pulled Arabella from her captor's arms.

"Go to the dressing room," he ordered.

"Julian, look out," she screamed as Bruce raised a pistol only to have it knocked out of his hand as Julian struck him on the chin, dropping him where he stood, the pistol falling from his nerveless grasp.

Despite her terror, Arabella scooped up the pistol, and holding it between both of her trembling hands, she aimed shakily at Nick, who had stumbled to his feet and was making another rush at Julian, only to be felled by a second powerful blow.

"What's amiss here? Good God!" Byron Capell, tall and bronzed and with a face that appeared to have taken more than one battering, strode forward. Assessing the situation in seconds, he aimed a powerful fist at Bruce, who had stumbled to his feet again. There was a loud crack as his fist connected with the latter's mouth, sending him unconscious to the ground again.

"Damned if I did not shatter his bone box," he said casually. " 'Twill be gruel and pap for him from now on, I should say." He turned toward Julian while several other coachmen, who had come to watch, grinned and muttered their approval. "I think it were better that these rogues not go free until we're a good distance—" He broke off as the little tiger from the curricle glared up at him.

"Wot do ye mean to do wi' their lordships?" he demanded shrilly, and glared as the coachmen burst into loud laughter.

"Their lordships, eh?" Mr. Capell also laughed. "What shall we do with them? What do you suggest, laddie?" With a lightning move, he reached down and picked up the boy.

"Lemme go . . . lemme go," the tiger struggled futilely in Mr. Capell's powerful grasp. "You'll be wanting to go with your master, I'm thinking." He glanced about him, still clutching the furious, struggling tiger. "A rope, a rope, my kingdom for a rope," he called.

"I'll fetch a rope," one of the coachmen offered, and hurried toward the post chaise Arabella had seen earlier.

"And a gag." Julian, who had been standing guard over the unconscious pair, bent down and hastily unwound Bruce's neckcloth.

"The very thing," Mr. Capell said approvingly. He looked down at the frantic, writhing tiger. "I fear 'tis my painful duty to . . ." He struck the boy under the chin, and as the child collapsed in his arms, he stuffed the neckcloth into his mouth and, receiving the rope from the coachman, trussed him up tightly. "Now," he said briskly, "I think we'll leave the three of them on the floor of the curricle and drive them to a . . . where?" He looked about him. "Does anyone have any suggestions for one who is not familiar with the territory?"

"Aye." One of the coachmen grinned. "There be a copse down the road a bit. And not far off that road, there be a deep ditch. It's 'ard by a pair o' elm trees. Leave'n there."

"Aye, bound and gagged like their tiger." Mr. Capell grinned. "Meanwhile, I'll send the curricle and horses home."

"But," a trembling Arabella said, "they might lay information against the company."

"I think," Mr. Capell said, "that it's more likely for their pride they'll talk of highwaymen to substantiate their tale. We'll leave them without their breeches and their boots and scatter their coins upon the roadway as if their attackers were suddenly affrighted."

"Aye." One of the coachmen nodded. "That'll serve'em good and proper. 'Tisn't the first time they've laid in wait for a pretty actress, and one poor lass killed 'erself after they let 'er go."

"Oh, God!" Arabella shuddered.

Julian moved forward to put an arm around her and then he said quickly, "Your gown, my dear."

Glancing down, she saw to her horror that it had been torn and hung open to her waist. She shrank back, putting up her hands, and in that moment, Julian lifted her up, holding her protectively as he said to Byron Capell, "I'd best get her back to the inn. Then, I will return and—"

"No." Mr. Capell grinned. "I'll see to the pair o' them, lad. These violent roles that have been my lot have given me a taste for villainy, which must ever go unrewarded since Tybalt dies and Jailor Lockit's fangs are drawn. Let me pretend that I have both Romeo and Captain MacHeath at my mercy."

There was low laughter among the watching coachmen, who now quickly made their way back to their vehicles as Arabella cried, "Oh, lovely, 'twill serve them right!" She blushed. "I mean . . ."

"I hope, wench, that you mean exactly what you said." Mr. Capell smiled at her. "And you are a brave girl for not turning tail and scurrying off like a frightened rabbit."

"She's not a rabbit, she's a lioness," Julian said softly.

"No, she is not," Arabella protested with a shiver. "If you'd not come, Julian, and you, sir . . ." She shivered again.

"As Shakespeare has said, 'All's well that ends well.' " Mr. Capell grinned. "Now let me remove this pair. Their ugly faces offend me."

"Come, Arabella." Julian carried her inside the dressing room, and putting her down on a couch, he looked about him. "There must be something you can wear."

"My costume," she said, blushing now. She had forgotten the condition of her gown.

"Good. Change into it. Do you need help?"

"No," she assured him.

"I will wait over here." He moved to the other side of the dressing room. "Let me know when you are ready."

Her costume was a poor exchange for her savaged gown, but at least it covered her, Arabella thought ruefully as she put on her cloak. "I am ready to go," she called shakily.

He was with her in a moment. Lifting her in his arms again, he said, "Put your arms around my neck, my dear."

"Oh, Julian, I can walk," she protested softly.

"I am sure you can, but I would rather carry you. Do you mind?"

It was too dark to see his features, the dressing room being illumined only by the moonlight streaming through a window, but there was a note in his voice she had never heard before. She said breathlessly, "No, I do not mind."

"We must have a long talk," he said. "But are you in the mood to converse?"

"Oh, yes, Julian, I am in the mood," she assured him, but her emotions were in a turmoil.

"We must go to an inn. I will bespeak a private room. Do you mind?"

As she had said before, she said again, "No, I do not mind."

The Red Lion was a few miles from the center of the city. It lay on one of the main highways and they arrived there shortly after eleven, having stopped to allow Arabella to discard her costume in exchange for a long-sleeved poplin gown in a green that matched her eyes. It was one of the garments she had brought from home and it was, she thought, less shabby than some of her other dresses. Unfortunately, its sleeves were fastened at the wrists with a row of small buttons, and she really needed Lizzie's help to slide them into their minute holes, but a glance into the latter's chamber had shown her that her abigail had not yet returned. She was obviously still with Jem and deserved a set-down, certainly, and would have it in the morning. She could not dwell on Lizzie's shortcomings now. Indeed, it was difficult to think about anything save her coming meeting with Julian. With that in mind, she managed the buttons, and such was her current state of excitement as she reached the innyard that she hardly remembered being lifted into a gig and cautioned to hold tightly to the strap at her side as Julian drove down the moonlit stretch of road.

It seemed to her that no more than a minute had passed before she was being ushered into a large sprawling inn, a few miles out of town. She wondered briefly if it were located anywhere near the ditch where Byron Capell had promised to deposit her would-be ravishers, but she forgot the actor and the men as Julian brought her into a small room furnished with a table and two chairs.

Candles glowed on the table and on a sideboard pushed against the wall. She noted a painting of fruit in a dish and another painting of a roiling sea and a storm-tossed ship. Then, Julian was helping her to a chair and taking another chair across from her. A moment later, a chambermaid had brought goblets and a bottle of wine. She curtsied and left the room, only to return with cakes, and then she was gone again and they were alone.

Julian said softly, "You must be hungry, my dear." He indicated the cakes and wine.

"No," Arabella breathed.

He smiled. "No more am I." Then he paused, regarding her quizzically before saying almost abruptly, "Arabella, you must leave us, you know."

"Leave?" she said in shock, realizing that she had hoped . . . But how had she dared cherish such a hope as that which, unbidden, had earlier slid across her mind?

Into the threatening chaos of her thoughts, Julian said, "You must leave us if . . ."

"If," he had said. And what had he meant by "if,"

a small word, a thin lifeline of a word. "If what?" she whispered.

He was silent a moment. Then, he said, "I have a question to ask you, but first there is something I must tell you. It is rather a long story. I hope you are not too tired to listen to me?"

"You know that I am not too tired," she dared to respond.

"I expect I do know that." He drew a long breath and expelled it shakily. "I must tell you about a wastrel who went through two fortunes at the tables —fortunes inherited from an uncle and an aunt. He did not waste the substance of his immediate family, because his father and his elder brother prevented that. And when the wastrel came to them, telling them that he was in deep trouble and stood in danger of debtor's prison because he could not pay his unfortunate creditors, his father, on the advice of his brother, refused to help him. It is possible that his father did not need his brother's persuasions, for he was not in sympathy with the wastrel and never had been.

"Consequently, our wastrel was clapped into debtor's prison, there to rot for three years, an object lesson, it was termed. In three years' time, the wastrel's debts would be paid and he would be freed. Accordingly, he went off to the King's Bench prison."

"Oh, how dreadful!" Arabella shuddered.

"Ah, you know of it?"

"I have heard of it," she said, remembering that Serena's father had been incarcerated in that same prison.

"It is better to hear of it than to experience it," he said wryly. "Our debtor was there for five months, and he knew that were he to stay for two years and seven months more, he might easily go mad—he who found out belatedly that he loved the green grass, the trees, the flowers, the snows of winter, the balmy breezes of summer, though for more time than he cared to admit, he had been seeing the servants replacing the melted candles at Brooks's, Boodles, and other hells as fortified by wine, he lost thousands and thousands of pounds to the sharpers or to the men who knew better than to play piquet and drink.

"But he was no longer at the tables, he was in the gray and gloomy confines of the prison." Julian shuddered. "There is an odor about the King's Bench that is like none other. It is composed of old clothes and dust and hopelessness . . ." He paused, his dark eyes seemingly turned inward, looking at the pictures he carried in his mind. "You might imagine that hopelessness being a state of mind, it would not have an odor, but it does.

"And this odor permeated our wastrel's clothes and it permeated his brain. He was near to despair when of a sudden he happened to fall into conversation with another prisoner. This prisoner was an actor, and he told the wastrel that when the company came to town, he would have his debts paid. He then said to the wastrel, 'You are very good-looking, sir, and you have a fine speaking voice. Mr. Gordon, who heads our company, is looking for a leading man. Would you consider . . . ?'

"Our wastrel looked at the actor as if he were mad. How dared he ask *him* if he would consider working in that most disreputable of professions? Our wastrel had seen actors only when he went backstage to pay his compliments to one or another pretty actress. Other than that, actors, in his opinion, were nothing!

"He was about to reject the offer in terms that would make the actor cringe and, indeed, make him very sorry that he had dared to approach a man of his birth and breeding with such an offer. The idea was unthinkable!

"Our wastrel's blood was a deep blue; our wastrel's ancestors had accompanied William the Conqueror from Normandy and they had fought at Agincourt and followed Charles the Second into exile and . . . But no matter, our wastrel was in prison and before him stretched what amounted to a lifetime, as far as he was concerned, so he swallowed his insults and told the actor he would think about it. He thought about it for exactly five minutes, then he said that if Mr. Gordon believed him actor material, he rather believed he might enjoy the work."

"Ah." Arabella smiled and clapped her hands.

Julian did not smile. He said only. "I see that the wastrel's decision has met with your approval, my dear?"

"Oh, yes, Julian, how could it not?" she breathed.

"I am glad of that, my dear, but I must tell you that the wastrel was not glad. Certainly, he was relieved when Mr. Gordon prevailed on those to whom he was in debt to take part payment and the rest in notes that the wastrel would redeem gradually, but it was close on seven months before he realized that he was enjoying the work and the people, and that he did not mind living frugally while he continued to pay off his creditors. It was about this time that an uncle of the wastrel returned to town, and since he was his mother's brother, he proved to be more in sympathy with his nephew than the paternal side of the family. He offered to pay off any remaining debts and set his nephew up in style again, and was quite surprised when the said nephew refused.

"However, the wastrel's uncle did not protest and the wastrel went on working with the company. He was doing very well when that company was joined by another reluctant performer—an actress. She did not have much acting ability, but she was beautiful and obviously she was of his own class, or close to it. I am afraid our wastrel was still a bit of a snob, even in those days. He soon realized that the beauty was a little less aristocratic than he had originally believed, but she was beautiful and she let him understand that she loved him and he thought he loved her. No, let us say that he did love her. He wanted her to be his wife and also he thought of leaving the company, even though he hated the idea of leaving almost as much as he loved our reluctant actress. He was still in the throes of making up his mind to propose when, fortunately for our wastrel, the reluctant actress dealt him a deep and painful blow. She left the company to marry well.

"Afterward, our wastrel castigated himself for not telling her the truth about his own background. He still had no money but he did have a title and he was sure that would appeal to her. Unfortunately, he had waited too long, and of course, he was much cast down. He told himself that he was brokenhearted. He told himself that he would never love again, but . . ." Julian flushed and paused. Then he continued, "That heart began to heal because he had met another . . ." He paused. "Oh, my dear Arabella, I do love you, you know."

Arabella stretched out her hand. On a breath, she murmured, "Do you?" and could say no more.

He took her hand, holding it warmly in both of his.
"Yes. I am not quite sure that I love you as much as I
once loved Serena, but I do know that were you to
leave the company, I would miss you quite dreadfully. You must leave, if you do not have a husband
to protect you." He paused and then said softly,
huskily, and even pleadingly, "I love you very much,
Arabella. I want to protect you. I want to be your
husband. Will you marry me, knowing my former
connection with Serena? And you must also know
that I can support you only through my acting. I have
paid my debts, but it has taken me close on three
years. I am only now—"

"Julian," she interrupted, "we can combine our
resources. Do not forget that I am acting also, and
yes, I will marry you, Julian. Oh, yes, oh, yes,
Julian," she whispered, and burst into tears. "I have
loved you for such a long time."

He rose swiftly, and coming around her side of the
table, he lifted her from her chair and held her close
against him. "My dearest, I thank you. I will try to
make you happy and . . . I could take you home, you
know. As I have told you, I am a younger son, but—"

"No." She put her fingers against his lips. "You
love what you are doing, Julian, and you are a
wonderful actor. I must tell you that I have wanted to
be an actress all of my life. Let us remain with the
Gordons, my dearest, please."

He said huskily, "I can give you very little, my
darling, but I can grant that wish. Of course, we will
stay."

"Oh, Julian," she breathed. "Oh . . ." And she
could say no more because he had kissed her. Then,
still holding her close, he rested his chin on her head.
"Oh, God, Arabella, have I said that I am not sure

how much I love you?'' In a voice thickened by passion, he continued, ''My dearest, I am a fool. I should have realized before now that there is room in my heart for only one woman, and that woman is you.'' He looked into her eyes, saying solemnly, ''Arabella, forsaking all others, I will love you and only you as long as there is breath in my body.''

''Oh, Julian, that is how I love you,'' she said passionately, and clinging to him, she warmed to yet another embrace.

Finally, he released her, saying reluctantly, ''I must take you back to the inn, my love. As I am an honorable man, I want you honorably, but I do not want to wait overlong. We are no great distance from Scotland—''

''Gretna Green,'' she interrupted excitedly.

''No, not Gretna Green. We have a week before we open in Richmond. We'll go to Scotland but we will be wed before a minister and a witness. I can secure a special license. Our wedding might not take longer than an anvil marriage, but it will be right and proper.'' He sighed. ''I wish I had a home to which I might take you.''

''Oh, Julian, my love,'' she whispered joyfully. ''*You* are my home.''

9

A ray of sunlight slid past an opening in the curtains and fell full on Arabella's face. It was warm against her eyes and it seeped between her long eyelashes, waking her. She blinked against the brightness and started to turn her head toward the pillow, but could not and was puzzled for a moment . . . and then, not puzzled. A tender smile curled her lips as she felt the long length of her husband beside her and guessed that he had fallen asleep on her hair. She did manage to turn her head slightly, and there he was next to her—close to her, a length of her bronze-gold hair spread beneath his head.

She flushed as she now saw that her nightgown was pulled down, showing most of her bosom. Then she felt a warmth not of the sun on her cheeks as she remembered the fourth of the nights she had spent with Julian. It had been more exciting than the third, just as the third had been more exciting than the second. As for the first, that had been puzzling and even a little frightening. She who had read a great deal about passion and had also pretended to it in one or another play had, she realized, never known what it meant—not really. And now words that had been only words to her had taken on a new meaning, and so had the motivations of the characters she played. She had never fully understood Juliet before or even little Maria, but united with Julian, passionately united, the unexplained was finally explained.

"Bella," he murmured drowsily.

"Yes, Julian," she whispered.

"Been wake long?"

"Just . . ."

"Love you, dreamed of you . . ."

"I love you, I dreamed of *you*."

He moved, releasing her hair. Propping himself up on one elbow, he stared down at her adoringly. "You are so beautiful," he said. "Beautiful face, beautiful body, beautiful hair . . . everything beautiful."

She moved against him. "You are beautiful, too."

"No," he protested.

"Yes," she insisted.

"A man's not beautiful."

"I think you are beautiful," she said stubbornly, running a finger down his cheek and feeling the bristles of his beard. Then her hand was captured and brought to his lips as he kissed each finger and brought his mouth down on the pulsing hollow at the base of her throat. The sensation, that indescribable sensation invaded her again while he continued to kiss her as passionately as if the ever-brighter sun was still last night's full moon.

An hour later, he stirred and sat up. "Richmond," he sighed.

"Yes." She would have sat up, too, but his hand pressed her back against the pillows as he smiled down at her adoringly.

"Are you there or am I only dreaming you, my dearest?" he asked.

She let her fingers play a little tattoo on his chest. "Is that part of your dream?"

He carried her hand to his lips and pressed a kiss in its palm. "Everything about you is part of my dream. By all rights and purposes, you should vanish like the moon vanishes with the coming of morning, but you must not, my love, for you would take my heart with you and a man must needs have his heart if he is to live."

"I will never vanish, Julian . . . never, never leave you," she promised. "But . . ."

"But . . . ?"

"But we must rise and attend rehearsal."

"Why?"

"Because we are actors and there is a rehearsal called."

"Oh, is there?" He nuzzled her cheek.

"There is." She pushed him away, saying determinedly, "Rise, Romeo."

"Very well, my love." In one fluid movement, he was up and out of bed and pulling her with him and into his arms again.

Since she knew him well enough not to argue, she did not.

On reaching the hall where they would perform that night, Richmond having no Theatre Royal, they came into an interior lighted only by a few candles, to receive greetings and applause from the assembled actors.

"And not even late," commented Mrs. Blackwell, who was to play the Nurse in *Romeo and Juliet*. "That's true professionalism for you, I must say."

"Aye," Mrs. Gordon agreed, and coughed. "Damn and blast," she added. "I have a frog in my throat that will not be dislodged but must needs turn my voice into croaks as if I were green and dwelling midstream on a lilypad," she paused, as laughter rippled through the company. Then, turning to Arabella, she said, "You will need to read Juliet, Mrs. Sherlay. It is to be hoped that I will be myself tonight."

"Mrs. Sherlay," Julian touched Arabella's arm.

Arabella gazed up at him vaguely, her eyes dreamy, "Yes?"

"I think you did not hear yon lady. You are to read Juliet at this rehearsal."

"I?" She regarded him incredulously. "Sure you must be funning me, Julian."

He waited until the laughter subsided. "I was but repeating what the lady just said, my love."

"I trust you know the role, my dear?" Mrs. Gordon asked.

"Know it, Mrs. Gordon? Oh, yes," Arabella breathed.

There was another burst of laughter from the cast and then the tapping of a stick on wood as Mr. Gordon said briskly, "Please begin at the top at Act One, Scene Three. We will take Juliet's entrance, ladies and gentlemen."

It was Saturday evening and the time was five minutes before the moment when Arabella, clad in Juliet's robes, was due to make her first entrance. She was in a ferment.

In essence, she could hear the murmurous audience in the auditorium, all who had been waiting to hear Mrs. Gordon and must be angry at the change in program announced before the beginning of Act One, an unwelcome prologue to the Prologue, she thought nervously.

Mrs. Gordon was a known quantity these ten years past. Her Juliet was a miracle of youth and beauty for all that she was thirty-five to her own nineteen. Furthermore, Julian would not even be beside her to wish her Godspeed with a kiss. He had done so already, but that was sometime back and now he was on the other side of the stage awaiting his next cue, waiting to play Romeo to her Juliet here in Richmond, which was not some small backwater town, but a large city, filled with knowledgeable, discerning, critical theatergoers, waiting dubiously to hear an unknown attempt a part she loved in a play she revered, but love and reverence were not enough!

She had to play Juliet, more than play her, breathe her, live her, and it was not a matter of reciting the potion scene, with which she had once astounded Julian, Julian, her husband, Julian, her Romeo. She was visited by a sudden suspicion that the part was Mrs. Gordon's wedding gift to them—and she must not fear it!

But was she ready? So much had happened of late: the lovely wedding in Scotland with the benign old minister reading herself and Julian the ceremony and accepting their vows and pronouncing them man and wife, and afterward, the incredible revelations of her wedding night and the knowledge that the man she loved loved her and not the chimera of Serena . . . But she must not think of Serena, changed from friend to enemy. She must concentrate on the part at hand: soon the balcony scene and—but there were so many hurdles to overcome—the potion scene, the death scene.

"Oh, God," she whispered, and then turned cold as Mrs. Eddington, as Lady Capulet, called impatiently, " 'Nurse, where's my daughter?' "

" 'Now, by my maiden head at twelve year old . . .

I bade her come, what love, what lady-bird. God forbid! Where's the girl . . . where's Juliet?' ''

Lifting up her long skirts, Juliet ran in lightly, saying, '' 'How now? Who calls?' ''

It was near the end of the play and Julian, who was Romeo, lay by Juliet's coffin. Arabella, having risen from her coffin, from Juliet's coffin, was seized with a terror for which she had no name, a terror out of context, out of the terror that she must soon simulate, looked upon his pale face, and closed eyes and thrust the dagger into her bodice, murmuring, '' 'This is thy sheath . . . there rest and let me die.' '' She fell on his warm body and shuddered, thinking of it, cold and in the tomb, then rejoiced to hear the pounding of his heart directly beneath her ear.

Later, after the applause, after the wildly excited reception in the greenroom, after the feast at a nearby tavern to celebrate a performance that everyone called a triumph, Julian and Arabella, happily alone, walked hand in hand to the inn, and later, lying together in the darkness of their chamber, made love. Then, as she pretended sleep, he said, "My darling, what is the matter?"

"The matter?" She moved closer to him and her fears increased, but she would not voice them. "Nothing, my love, save nerves. From time to time, I feared I would not be able to finish the role. I thought I must call upon Mrs. Gordon to step into the part."

"I do not believe you," he said almost sternly. "From start to finish, you were perfection, and do not tell me that you are unaware of that! An actor always knows." He dropped a kiss on her cheek.

"There's something else that troubles you, my dearest."

"I do not understand you, Julian." She tried to speak lightly over the pounding in her throat, over the inexplicable fear that had visited her off and on throughout the evening and seemed even greater now.

"I still do not believe you. Why are you frightened?" he demanded edgily.

"I do not know," she half-sobbed. "I have no name for it. Maybe I have become too happy. It is dangerous to be too happy, I think."

"Oh, my love, my love," he said huskily, and was silent as he kissed her. Then he said, "If there is danger here, let me experience it, too. Indeed, let me experience it all the days of my life, for surely never did danger wear so beautiful a face and form."

She started to protest, started to warn him of . . . what? She did not know and could not think, for Julian had wound his arms around her and rapture replaced all coherent thought.

"Love, love, wake up, do."

Opening drowsy eyes, Arabella blinked against brightness and was surprised. It had been a gray day yesterday, driving from Norwich. She smiled up at her husband, taking in every line and curve of his handsome face. Nearly four months of marriage had not dimmed her excitement at waking to his gentle summons and to his face so near to her own. However, there was a difference this morning. He was already dressed, and as usual, he looked as if a fashionable valet had turned him out. No one seeing him would have dreamed that it was he who had starched his neckcloth and pressed his coat and his unmentionables and even ironed his shirt. She, who had finally learned to do without the services of Lizzie, now employed as a dresser in the theater and soon to marry Jem, could also press her gowns, but the process invariably took longer.

She said contritely, "I expect I overslept again."

"You might have had I not woken you, Miss Slug-a-bed," he said teasingly.

She pulled a face. "Well, I will be up in seconds. Did the girl bring water?"

"A tubful, and it is still warm."

"Oh, lovely."

"And there's tea."

"Better and better. Why are you so good to me, Julian?"

"Because I love you." He dropped another kiss on the top of her head.

"No, here," she protested, and pointed to her lips and giggled as he obliged. "Have I told you that I adore you?" she demanded as he drew back.

"No," he sighed.

She glared at him. "Mr. Sherlay, when have I not told you?"

"This morning, Mrs. Sherlay."

"May I tell you now?"

"You must."

"Very well, I adore you, adore you, adore you."

"My sweetest girl." He kissed her lightly and would have moved away had she not stretched out her arms and put them around his neck, needing to cling to him because on falling asleep the previous night, she had had a feeling she had not experienced since her marriage. The fears she had felt so strongly then had evaporated and she had been able to put them from her mind, but now, inexplicably, they had

returned. They would give color to her performance
as Juliet that evening, and she hoped that, as before,
they meant nothing. Of course, they might be
predicated on something she planned to tell him. She
had been sure of it only yesterday, but with Julian
due to play Romeo in the same theater where David
Garrick had made his debut in 1741, she had not
wanted to say anything.

Julian was not overly afflicted with nervousness,
but he would be nervous this night, mainly because
the audience in Ipswich, Mr. Gordon had said
somewhat caustically, measured each actor who
played there by that formidable yardstick named
David Garrick. Indeed, there were those among the
audience who did not abstain from tossing produce
and rotten eggs and took a goodly supply of both, in
case an actor did not measure up to the great man.

"My angel, you are looking uncommon sober,"
Julian said.

"It is a sobering thought to play opposite to an
actor who is even greater than David Garrick." She
smiled, willing those fears to stop plaguing her.

"Oh, what utter nonsense you do speak," he
protested, and pulling back the covers, he said, "You
must rise, my angel. Not only do we need to ascertain
the lay of the theater, but I wish to walk with you
through the town, as we always do."

"How many towns, how many, how many?" She
smiled at him as she slid out of bed. "I have lost
count. Besides, I never think about them as towns or
cities. They are always stages: wide stages, narrow
stages, strong stages, weak and creaky old stages.
'All the world's a stage and all the men and women
merely players . . .' "

"Precisely, but never 'merely' when you are playing upon those stages, my love."

"Not me. You."

"I'll not argue." He moved to her, and before she knew what he had in mind, he whisked off her nightshift, carried her to the tub, and deposited her in the water, unmindful of her shrieks.

"Oh, you!" She made a face at him and lifted the sponge threateningly. "I have a mind to throw this at you and ruin your sartorial beauty."

"Use the other half of your mind and do not," he ordered, assuming a threatening stare. "We do not have all the time in this world. Besides"—his frown vanished—"I have a particular desire to walk through Ipswich with my beloved on my arm and show her off to David Garrick's envious shade. He *will* envy me, you know. Peg Woffington could never have equaled you."

"Idiot," she said lovingly, and as if he had willed it, she forgot her fears.

The applause at the Theatre Royal was tremendous, and not one actor had sustained so much as an apple core hurled in contempt. The Juliet, draped in grave clothes, bowed and bowed again, holding fast to the hand of her Romeo. She was full now of the secret she longed to impart to him. Unfortunately, facing her was the ordeal of their coming appearance in the greenroom. She wished heartily that it were possible to avoid it. Unfortunately, that was one ritual they dared not overlook. They had received a wonderful welcome from an audience known to be notoriously hard to please, and they must express their gratitude. She prayed fervently that they would not be delayed overlong.

Alas, for her hopes, Arabella thought some thirty minutes later as she stood in the greenroom. This had proved to be one of those hectic nights when, already weary from acknowledging the plaudits of the influential members of the community, she was now surrounded by a group of would-be ardent young men who were teasing her, praising her, and also embarrassing her with lewd comments and sly suggestions that she was very glad Julian, himself surrounded by the coterie of admiring females who appeared at his every performance, could not hear. However, there was one man who stood back from her importunate admirers. He had been standing in that same spot for quite a while and she had caught his eyes on her. Indeed, she had a feeling that for the considerable amount of time that he had been watching her, his gaze had never shifted, his reptilian gaze, she thought uncomfortably. It was a look that both angered and frightened her. Each time she had inadvertently met that unwavering stare she had been aware of a compelling intensity, unlike anything she had ever seen before.

Against her will, she found herself wondering who he might be. Obviously, he was a member of the *ton*. He was elegantly clad and he was older than the young men around her. He did not look like a citizen of the town, nor had he, she felt sure, come in on the stage coach. He would have his own curricle or post chaise or coach. She stiffened, for he had suddenly lifted a quizzing glass and was now surveying her out of an eye that was magnified in a most unsettling manner. Feeling extremely disquieted, she turned back to the teasing youths about her, tiredly receiving their extravagant compliments. Yet, before she had shifted her gaze, she had glimpsed an amused smile and was, for some reason she could not quite fathom, reminded of a cat, a predatory cat crouching at a mouse hole.

No, she did understand that analogy. His eyes, even without the aid of his quizzing glass, caught and compelled. She sensed that he was a man with a strong will, and with that conclusion, her nervousness increased. She had a sudden impulse to quit the greenroom immediately. She shot a lightning glance around the room and saw the large portrait of a bewigged Garrick as Hamlet. She did not see her husband at this moment, and then Mrs. Gordon was at her side and with her was the man she had not liked.

"My dear Mrs. Sherlay," she said with obvious fanfares in her tone. "This gentleman, the Marquess of Dorne, has expressed a strong desire to make your acquaintance."

"Your lordship." Arabella raised her eyes reluctantly to his face and was once more uncomfortably reminded of that cat. His eyes were a strange color, a sort of yellow green. They gleamed like those of a beast in the jungle, she decided nervously as she abandoned her earlier comparison of cat.

She reluctantly stretched out her hand and he kissed it; his lips were cold, and on raising his head, he still held her hand. He said, "I wish to tell you, ma'am, that I have scarce seen such remarkable acting even in London. You *are* Juliet."

"There, my love," Mrs. Gordon, nice, unenvious

Mrs. Gordon, said proudly. "She learned her role under my aegis, your lordship. She has acted nowhere but in this company."

"I am quite aware of that, ma'am. I would have most certainly remembered her, had I seen her before. She is quite, quite unforgettable."

"You are kind to say so, my lord," Arabella murmured, liking him even less and wishing strongly that Mrs. Gordon had not seen fit to introduce him. However, second thoughts intervened to inform her that the lady had had no choice but to obey this man. It was quite obvious that he compelled obedience.

He said, "On the contrary, Mrs. Sherlay, I am not kind. I am never kind. I am quite unforgivably honest, and at all times. I know what I like and I know what I dislike." His lordship smiled, revealing strong white teeth that, Arabella thought, should have been fangs. She controlled a shudder and quite actively willed him away, but of course, he did not go.

Mrs. Gordon did go, smilingly and murmuring about someone across the room needing her attention. Oddly enough, no one else came to congratulate her. Arabella had a strange feeling that Lord Dorne had willed them all away while he continued to stare at her with his beast's eyes, compelling her own reluctant gaze.

He said, "I had never expected to find so fair a flower here. I thought the managers in London had plucked them all, but they have been sadly remiss. No matter, that can be rectified and quickly. You will come with me tonight, of course. And within the week I will take you to my friend who is the manager of the Haymarket. He will mount a production of

Romeo and Juliet for you. Get your cloak, girl, and let us be off.''

She regarded him incredulously. ''I cannot come with you, my lord.''

He frowned. ''Do not be missish, my dear. Of course, you must come with me. I live not too far distant. And I mean what I say about your future career in the theater.''

His air of command and his apparent belief that she must obey him without question both frightened and angered her. She said freezingly, ''You will excuse me, my lord, but I am not in the least interested in anything that you might choose to do for me, and I have no intention of going anywhere with you.'' Much to her annoyance, her voice quavered where it ought to have commanded.

He raised thin eyebrows. ''Even were I to tell you that I can oversee your career to the point that you will be the most famous actress in London and, rather than wasting your brilliant talents on this provincial audience, be appearing before the Prince Regent and his mother, the Queen of England? Does that not interest you, my dear? Do not tell me differently. You are not quite that accomplished an actress.'' He put his hand on her arm, grasping it tightly, hurtfully. ''Now, I beg you will cease these missish airs. They do not appeal to me. Come, I say. My coach is outside, my love.''

''I am not your love, your lordship, and no, it does not interest me. I am quite sure that I will appear in London in due time—if I choose to do so.''

His eyes widened and then narrowed. He smiled, a most unpleasant smile. ''A slut with the airs of a queen, a most interesting anomaly.''

"You are pleased to be insulting, my lord. Yet, I do not need to suffer these insults. I must ask that you please release my arm," Arabella said coldly.

His grip tightened. "I begin to think that you do not know to whom you are speaking, my girl. Do not put on these airs with me. You are much to my taste and you will not regret the arrangement I am offering. I am the Marquess of Dorne and I am offering you carte blanche."

"And I am refusing it, your lordship. I am impressed neither by your offer nor by yourself. I do not enjoy rudeness from any individual, high or low, and now I must ask that you please take your hand from my arm."

His brows drew together, his grasp became even more hurtful. Then he laughed. "I must say that you are an impudent little doxy. Oh, I know you call yourself an 'actress,' my lass, and as I have said you are extremely gifted, but show me the actress who will not sell her services."

"I am that actress, my lord," she returned coldly. "I am married, and even if I were not, I would not go with you. I do not wish to go with you. I do not like you. I find you insufferably rude and overbearing. Now let me go."

His hurtful hold remained on her arm. He said, "In due time, my love, but first, this night, or what remains of it, belongs to me—or rather, to *us*." He started toward the door, pulling her with him, and it seemed to Arabella that no one appeared to be aware of his actions. If they were, they gave no sign of noticing as he started forward, dragging her with him. Then, of course, she had no alternative save to call loudly, to shriek, "Julian, Julian, help me, Julian."

In that moment, it seemed to her that the room had grown amazingly silent. The laughter and chatter were stilled and suddenly Julian, who had been surrounded by a group of admiring females, hurried to her side, his eyes narrowed as he regarded his lordship, who had still not troubled to relax his grip on Arabella's arm and who now appeared mightily amused.

Julian now fixed his eyes on his wife's frightened face. "What is amiss, my love?"

"Nothing is amiss," his lordship murmured before Arabella could respond. "I want the wench. She pleases me and I will see that she—"

"You cannot have her, my lord. I will thank you to release my wife," Julian said icily.

"Oh, you're the husband? I will be delighted to pay you—" He ceased speaking at that moment because Julian had struck him hard across the face.

"You will please release my wife," he said, and subsequently effected that release himself by thrusting the marquess back and putting his arm around his trembling wife.

Lord Dorne staggered slightly, but righted himself quickly. His eyes had narrowed. He said softly, but with the hiss of a serpent in his speech, or so it seemed to a terrified Arabella, "That was most unwise, young man."

"Julian," Arabella mouthed.

"Swords or pistols, your lordship," Julian said.

Lord Dorne's beast's eyes had widened, and to Arabella's mind they held the soulless look of a tiger in a menagerie. He said incredulously, "Do you imagine that I would demean myself to fight with the likes of you? You should be given ten lashes for your impudence, you young scoundrel."

"Am I to infer that your lordship is afraid to fight me?" Julian demanded contemptuously, his words falling into the pool of silence that had supplanted the laughter and the chatter.

"Afraid of an impudent rascal, a nobody from nowhere such as yourself?" the marquess demanded furiously.

"Are you, my lord?" Julian demanded coolly.

"Oh, Julian, no, please, no." Arabella had found her voice. "Please, he—"

He did not look at her. He continued to stare coldly at the marquess. "I am waiting for your response, my lord. Are you afraid to voice it, then?"

"No, damn you, I am not afraid." Lord Dorne was smiling now. "I am not used to fighting with knaves of your ilk, but I think you must be taught a lesson and I am pleased that I am the one chosen to do it."

"Swords or pistols, my lord?" Julian questioned calmly.

"Swords, of course. It will give me considerable pleasure to cut you before I kill you. Even if you should survive, I think you will no longer be a Romeo to please the ladies. I think your next role will be Caliban."

A horrified murmur swept the room and one of the ladies began to cry. However, Julian did not appear to be impressed by his lordship's threats. He said merely, "You will need to name the meeting place. I am unfamiliar with this territory."

"I shall be delighted. There is a stretch of land where fairs are often held. It lies beyond the city gates. I will advise your seconds of the exact location and we will meet at dawn—when I shall be pleased to, er, draw your claret."

In only a few moments—or it might have been

longer, Arabella was not sure—they were away from the theater. Julian had stopped only long enough to name his second, who was, of course, his best friend in the company, Byron Capell, bereft of his usual grin. He had looked grave and angry as he agreed to confer with his lordship's seconds.

"I will come for you at dawn," he told Julian. "His lordship will furnish the rapiers."

"Be sure you examine them closely," Julian had advised. He had actually smiled as he added, "I do not wish to be confronted with a venom-tipped blade such as that which Hamlet faced."

Arabella, walking beside Julian, could say nothing, and he was similarly silent. Then, much to her amazement, she found herself at the inn. A few more moments, and they were in their chamber. Then, as Julian closed and locked the door, she ran to him, tears pouring down her cheeks. "Oh, God, Julian," she sobbed. "I am so sorry . . . so sorry."

"Why are you sorry, my dearest?" He drew her into his arms.

"If I'd not spoken to him . . . I saw him earlier and did not like his looks or the way he looked at me. I should not have spoken to him, not even after Mrs Gordon brought him to me. I did not want to speak to him but there was nothing I could do. He caught my arm . . ." She paused, realizing that she was not making much sense.

Julian said grimly, "He will be sorry for his actions, my love, and sorrier for offering to buy the services of my bride."

"But, Julian"—tears filled her eyes—"he could kill you."

"Shhhh, shhhh, my very sweetest." He covered her tear-wet face with kisses. Then, raising his head, he said, "I have told you practically everything there is to know about me, my beautiful, but I do not believe I have told you that I am an excellent swordsman. I have had the best masters in London and I have profited by my lessons, I can assure you."

"He said that he would cut your face."

"I heard what he said, but the loudest threats quite often prove to be the emptiest boasts. He wanted to frighten me, you see." Anger filled his tones again. "I think, perhaps, he wanted me to withdraw from the duel."

She shook her head. "But, of course, you could not have done so."

"Oh, my love, I do thank you for being so understanding. Of course, I could not. And now, my angel, in case anything unforeseen happens—"

"No, no, no, it will not," she sobbed, throwing her arms around him and holding him protectively against her. "It will not."

"Hear me, my dearest, it is important that you should listen to me," he said quite sternly.

She had never heard that note in his voice. She drew away from him, feeling ashamed of her outburst. With a strong effort, she downed her panic and said, "I am sorry, Julian, dearest, tell me what you wish."

"I do not want you to stay with the company if I cannot protect you. I want you to go to my uncle."

"Lord Calthrope." She nodded.

"Yes, I would send you to my father, but as I have told you, we are not in sympathy."

"I would not want to go to your father, Julian," she said, swallowing a large lump in her throat. "I wish never to meet your father or your brother. They are—"

"Enough, love," he said softly. "Do not vent your spleen on them, I pray. My uncle ought to be in London at this time. I will write out his direction. As I have told you, he has a soft spot for his disgraceful nephew and I know he will be pleased to harbor his bride."

"Oh, Julian," she sobbed. "Do not speak as if you anticipated . . . Oh, God, I wish we could leave this place tonight. Honor or no honor!"

"No, you do not," he said gravely. "I could not live without honor, nor could you share a coward's bed. Could you?"

As she met his eyes, an answer trembled on her tongue, but she swallowed it and reluctantly shook her head, not because she believed it, but because she knew that this was the answer he craved. "No, Julian," she sighed.

"My beautiful, my brave little liar." He kissed her. "There speaks the woman I am proud to call my wife. Now, my sweetest girl, we have at least five hours before dawn. I have made arrangements with Byron. He will come to wake me when it is time."

"Time," she echoed, but held back her threatening tears. "Let us go to bed, Julian, dearest," she said calmly. "You will need your sleep."

She did not believe she would sleep, but warmed by her husband's body and relaxed by his passionate lovemaking, she could not fight the drowsiness that swept over her. Because, of late, she had been prone to fall into heavy slumbers, she was, much to Julian's relief, still heavily asleep when Byron Capell came to fetch him, and she remained asleep while they moved softly out of the chamber and down the stairs. In a few moments, they were traveling up an almost deserted road under a paling sky wherein the sun was still a dark-red streak across the eastern horizon.

"Milady, milady!" A gentle but determined hand was on Arabella's shoulder, urging her to wake.

Coming out of a heavy sleep, she blinked against brightness and to her surprise, found Lizzie, her one-time abigail, standing over her. She dimly perceived an anxious-looking Byron Capell standing near the door.

She sat up, pulling the sheet about her, staring at them confusedly. Then memory flooded into her mind, bringing with it terror. "Julian," she cried. "Where is Julian? Oh, God, you'll not tell me that the duel, that he—"

"No, milady," Lizzie said hastily and soothingly.

"No, my dear." Mr. Capell added his voice to that of the abigail. "The duel is at an end and Julian was unhurt."

She looked around the chamber. "Then, where is he? Why is he not here?"

"He has been arrested," Mr. Capell said angrily. "Julian has been accused of attempted murder. His accuser is the Marquess of Dorne, who is, most unfortunately, also a justice of the peace and empowered to try criminals here. He has said that Julian will be sentenced to be transported for endangering the life of a peer."

"But that is a lie, a damned lie," Arabella cried. "It was he who forced the duel on Julian."

"No, my dear," Mr. Capell sighed. "It was our Julian issued the challenge to the marquess."

"But you know why," she cried hotly.

"Aye, we all know, but Julian is an actor and his lordship is a peer, a peer who is recovering from a punctured shoulder and a severed tendon in his right arm. Unless he is ambidextrous, he'll not be dueling soon again.''

She dismissed the description of his lordship's wounds. ''Can I see Julian?'' she cried.

''I think, yes, you may see him, but we must go to London, to Julian's uncle. I will accompany you—and the sooner we leave, the better it will be for him.''

''You are positive that Julian was not hurt?'' Arabella demanded.

''He did not sustain so much as a scratch, my dear.'' Mr. Capell permitted himself a brief smile. ''He was grace itself, consummate grace against the dogged onslaught of a maddened bull—damn his lordship to hell.''

''And is imprisoned now,'' Arabella cried. ''How many days to London?''

''I would think that, given good weather and long hours on the road, we could reach the city in two days at the most.''

''Two days there and two back, and time when I must see his uncle—and my aunt, if he cannot help. Oh, God, is there no way of providing bail?'' Arabella demanded.

''They'll not allow bail. There are laws against dueling.''

She said slowly, ''How well are you acquainted with Julian, Mr. Capell? Has he ever told you . . .''

He nodded, saying quickly, ''Yes, I know all about him.''

''Then, if he is of the same rank . . .''

''That would need to be proven. To the constable and the jailer, he is naught but an actor—and he carries no papers to prove otherwise.''

"You could speak for him. I, too."

"I am an actor," he said wryly, "and you, my love, are an actress—and his wife. The marquess is a powerful man in this area."

"When may I see him?" she demanded.

"As soon as you are dressed, I will take you to the constable."

"When does the stage coach leave for London?"

"At one in the afternoon, but we'll not need to board it. I have permission from the Gordons to take their post chaise."

"Oh, that is good of them," she cried thankfully.

"They are fond of you, my dear, and fond of Julian. Mrs. Gordon has empowered me to tell you that she will do with substitutes until you and Julian return, but that you are to be assured that the company will be glad to welcome you back."

"Oh, how kind of her. I would bid her farewell, but—"

"No," he interrupted urgently. "We must leave as soon as possible."

"I will not go without seeing Julian," Arabella cried. She turned to Lizzie. "Will you come with us, then, my dear, to London?"

"I'd never let you go without me, milady," the girl said staunchly.

Her eyes ablaze with fury, Arabella stood in the anteroom of the jail, a crumbling old building with barred windows fronting the town square. It was very warm in the chamber, it would be even warmer in the cells, she knew. She said, as she had said before, "But I tell you, I am his wife." She glared at

the imperturbable and unprepossessing man who sat
at the desk.

"I demand that you let me see my husband!"

He raised cold eyes set in pouched sockets and let
them wander over her body from toes to head, before
he said, "Whether you is or whether you isn't—"

"She is his wife," Lizzie, standing beside Arabella,
cried furiously.

The constable eyed her as well. "Either way, 'is
lordship's given strict orders that the criminal's not to
be allowed visitors. An' that, er, ladies, is that."

Arabella stamped her foot. "He is not a criminal. It
was a duel."

"Duels is forbidden by law. In my book 'twas
attempted murder, 'n if 'is lordship was to die . . ."

"He will not die. There's no chance of that, though
I wish he might," she cried.

The constable's brows lowered. "More outa you,
ma'am, and you'll be 'eld as accessory under the
law."

Arabella drew herself up. "You could not," she
said icily. Then, as more words threatened to escape
from her, she turned and left, followed by a relieved
Lizzie. It was only when she was back in the post
chaise that she said despairingly to Mr. Capell,
"They'd not let me see him. What are they doing to
him?"

"There's nothing they can do, save put him in
chains." Mr. Capell frowned.

"Chains in that hot stifling place? Oh, God!"

"Come," Mr. Capell said briskly, "let us be on our
way. It is a clear day and we will be able to make good
time before nightfall."

"Yes, let us go," she agreed. She thought of Lady

Olivia, banished from her mind for the better part of a year with her father and Serena, and she felt oddly comforted. If Julian's uncle would not heed them, her aunt would.

Though on occasion there were clouds in the sky, no rain descended, nor were there unseemly delays on the roads or lengthy waits at the turnpikes. Mr. Capell also knew what he described as a "clean inn," the Golden Horse, and they spent the night there. As he had promised, the beds were comfortable and the linen clean. The food was passable and thanks to Jem's skillful manipulation of the ribbands and the help of young Will Wilkins, an apprentice actor, they made very good time and reached London by eleven in the evening of their second day on the road.

Since it was too late to seek out either her aunt or Julian's uncle, and mindful of her own weariness, Arabella let herself be persuaded to spend the night at a lodging house in Chelsea, one much frequented by the acting fraternity. She was shown to a small, neat chamber with whitewashed walls, furnished by a narrow bed, but with clean linen, and if the mattress sagged, it was not uncomfortable.

However, as Arabella was quick to assure herself, it might have been made of slats and covered with burlap and she would have found it equally welcome. Indeed, she was so weary that she was only vaguely aware of Lizzie's ministrations. It was only when the girl left the room that despair settled down on Arabella like a dark cloud. She was racked by fear and by tormenting doubts, mainly centering on Lord Dorne and whatever villainy he might perpetrate in her absence. Yet, what could he do, lying in his bed of pain? And why had she not been allowed to visit Julian? Could they employ torture in this day and age? That was unlikely, but Julian would suffer enough, locked in a small airless cell in this hot weather.

"If only . . ." she murmured, wishing that she had been able to give him the news, the wonderful news she had been saving until they would have retired to their chamber that night, that fatal night when triumph had become tragedy.

Tragedy.

She shuddered, envisioning tragedy's face, a mask with a turned-down mouth, a face of sorrow and doom.

"What will he do to Julian?" she whispered.

She remembered his threat of transportation to New South Wales and shuddered. Julian could not be sent to that wild, inhospitable shore where criminals disembarked to serve sentences by laboring on the roads and performing other harsh manual tasks. That was no place for Julian, her elegant, gently-bred young husband. But were he forced to go, she would follow him. She would follow him to hell, she thought fiercely, but he must not risk hell because he had saved his wife from her would-be seducer, because he had repulsed and wounded that same miscreant.

His uncle must help him.

"You must, you must, you must," she added, addressing in her mind a shadowy someone, Lord Calthrope, the brother of Julian's long-dead mother. Had she not been long dead, surely she must have interceded for her son, but it was late to dwell on that and he did not need a mother now—he had a wife.

10

"But I must see his lordship," Arabella said to the tall, gray-haired, portly butler who stood in the front entrance of the tall, slate-colored house on Charles Street, as unmoving as a block of granite.

"His lordship is not astir yet, and he's not available to the likes of you, miss," he said insultingly.

"Wot do you mean addressin' 'er ladyship in such terms, you beetle-nosed old—" Lizzie shrilled.

"Lizzie, be silent, please," Arabella said reprovingly. Then, in a voice she vainly tried to keep from shaking, she continued, "I tell you that I have come from Lord Calthrope's nephew, Mr. Julian Sherlay, and I must see him. Mr. Sherlay is in jail and—"

"And not for the first time," the butler retorted rudely, his insolent gaze on her shabby garments. Obviously, he regarded her much as he would regard a beggar seeking alms.

"Let there be an end to poverty," Julian had said before the *Romeo and Juliet*. "I want to take you home. You must not live this way. How long is it since you have had a new cloak or a new gown?"

"I do not want to live any other way. I love this life," she had assured him, and seen gladness in his eyes, for, needless to say, he loved it, too. And would this life he loved be his death, or rather, would she be his death?

"Please, I must see his lordship," Arabella cried, uncharacteristically trying to push her way past the stolid, solid mass of the butler.

"His lordship is not home to you, now or ever." The butler thrust her back and slammed the door in her face.

"Oh, milady," Lizzie cried.

Fury brought Arabella's hand to the knocker, but she took it away. "We must go to my aunt," she said. "I should have gone there ere now, but I did not want to take the time. Come, Lizzie, let us hurry."

She came down the walk to the waiting post chaise, a vehicle as shabby as her own person, she realized, seeing it through the butler's haughty gaze, seeing her thin gold wedding ring, seeing her mended garments. She and Julian had been fugitives from a life they had both loathed, preferring the freedom of the roads and the joy of their despised profession. Yet, in a sense they were actors both on and off the stage. She could even say that they had been playing at being players. Certainly, they had been less successful off stage than on. Neither had been quite able to develop the humility required for their daily roles. It had not been Arabella, the actress, who had repulsed the marquess; it had been Lady Arabella, who had found within herself a strong desire to put this man in his place—a place no higher than her own! And it had not been Julian, the humble actor, who had challenged Lord Dorne to a duel; it had been Julian, the aristocrat, who spoke to Dorne in terms he understood. And now both she and her husband stood in danger of being punished for a—

Could it be called a betrayal of their heritage? And Julian faced a most terrible punishment if help were not quickly forthcoming! She read that in Mr. Capell's anxious gaze.

She said, "We *will* go to my aunt." She spoke as determinedly as if she were sure that Lady Olivia still remained in London. If she did not . . . Well, that would be part of her own punishment for cutting herself off so completely from her entire family, but she would not consider such a possibility. She added, "I will give you her direction. She lives not far from here—she is staying in a house on Grosvenor Square."

Over a spread of tea, cakes, and clotted cream, Lady Olivia stared at Arabella out of tear-wet eyes and put a damp square of cambric to them, as she had quite often since her niece's arrival and her hurried explanation of her presence in the city.

"Eight months and married and your poor young husband in such terrible straits," she said distractedly. "Yes, yes, something must be done. I wish my brother . . . He has been racked by anxiety, my dear. He started to search for you and would have continued were it not for his—for Serena's illness."

"Her illness?" Arabella asked, curious in spite of her own terrible anxieties.

"After you left . . ." Lady Olivia shook her head. "I know I should not burden you with it now, but your father was much exercised over the matter. He made inquiries of all the nearest families—whether anyone had spoken to you—and of course, young Humphrey had. He told Adrian that he believed it was partially Serena's fault that you had gone. He said that his wife had told him Serena was anxious that you be out of the house willy-nilly, and had persuaded Lord Kinnard to offer for you again—and, of course, Adrian remembered her persuading of himself. There was a confrontation, and your father, I fear, lost his temper. He seized her by the shoulders and shook her hard. Then, he told her that she was evil and conniving, that she had repaid your own love for her in very poor coin, and that he wanted nothing more to do with her! Of course, when he later described the scene to me, he was most contrite. He had not meant it: he loved Serena, loves her still. But she was cast into the very deepest despair."

"Indeed?" Arabella raised her eyebrows. "Or was she merely acting? Her acting off stage cannot be faulted, as I have learned to my sorrow."

Lady Olivia said regretfully, "I used to pray that you would come to your senses as far as Serena was concerned, my dear. And certainly you have. It was to be expected, of course, after all your unhappiness."

Arabella regarded her in surprise. "You speak as if you were not quite in sympathy with me, Aunt Olivia."

"Oh, no, child, I am entirely in sympathy with you. I cannot blame you for being skeptical, but let me assure you that skepticism is not warranted here. Serena is no actress on or off the stage. It appears that she felt intimidated by you and thought you did not approve of her marriage. She believed that you were trying to show her that she was not worthy of your father's love, and that was why she turned against you."

"But that is ridiculous," Arabella cried.

"Of course, it was ridiculous. It arose out of her own very real lack of self-worth. After her confrontation with your father, she tried to leap from her bedroom window and was caught in the nick of time by a servant who happened to come into her chamber unexpectedly."

"And," Arabella said coldly, "told of her desperate act by that same servant, my father realized that she truly loved him and rushed to soothe her? If she is not an actress, she must have some talent for playwriting."

Lady Olivia shook her head. "No, he was not even home at the time. He remained angry, he told me, and she fell into a dangerous melancholy, very dangerous, Arabella. It still lingers in the back of her mind, I fear. Your father began to feel very sorry for her, but pity is not love. Matters between them are improving, but they are not the same. I doubt they ever will be. Adrian is not cruel, but he was disappointed in Serena—as I think you were disappointed. And he has found that her beauty is not matched by wit. Her conversation was always commonplace, and now she tends to be rather vague. However, she responds well to kindness and Adrian is doing his best to be kind to her—but she wearies him."

"I see," Arabella spoke almost perfunctorily. "I beg you, Aunt Olivia, let us not dwell on Serena any longer. We must see Julian's uncle." She sighed as she thought of the time wasted while she argued with Lord Calthrope's butler and subsequently with David, her aunt's butler. He had been similarly ungracious to the shabby young woman at the door.

Fortunately, she described her aunt's appearance to his satisfaction and he had grudgingly summoned her ladyship and then had embarrassedly watched the shabby visitor being lovingly embraced by his employer. He had also seen her gracious greeting of

Lizzie. Currently, Mr. Capell was also with them, eyeing the beautifully appointed chamber with an interest bordering upon awe.

He now added his voice to Arabella's persuasions. "It is very important that we see his lordship as soon as possible, milady. The assizes will be meeting during the first week in July."

"Oh, God, so soon?" Arabella cried. "You did not tell me that!"

"I did not wish to alarm you," he said carefully, "but we must return as soon as possible."

"Yes, we must, that horrid man, I do not trust him," Arabella cried.

"We could leave today," Lady Olivia said. "I could speak for Julian."

"Begging your pardon, milady, but it were better his uncle stood for him," Mr. Capell said. "It is not that they wouldn't take your word but . . ."

"But they might not," she finished. "His uncle's word would certainly carry more weight. And what of his father and brother? Where are they?"

"They live some distance from Ipswich," Arabella said. "And they are not in sympathy. His brother . . ." she frowned. "But enough. Aunt Olivia, were you to call on Lord Calthrope, you'd not be turned away certainly."

Lady Olivia was silent a moment. Then she said, "Actually, my child, I think it were better if I dispatched a note asking his lordship to come here." Seeing distress flare in Arabella's eyes, she added hastily, "It would give you time to change your garments. We are much of a size, my love, and I have a gown that might suit you—a cloak as well—and both are as yet unworn."

"I could not take them—" Arabella began.

"Nonsense!" Lady Olivia spoke more briskly than was usually her wont. "You will take the gown and look your best for his lordship."

"You must, milady," Lizzie cried, and then reddened. "I mean—"

"You mean that you agree with me." Lady Olivia smiled at the girl. "Pride goeth before a fall and initial impressions are important. You have told me of your regrettable experience at the house of Lord Calthrope. We will hope that upon meeting you, he will dismiss his importunate butler."

"And will you dismiss your own?" Arabella demanded.

"I might have so done, and gladly, were he my servant to dismiss," Lady Olivia said with an edge to her tone. "But he is in the service of my friend Lady Agnes, whose house this is. She is currently visiting a friend in Scotland, and thank God, she was not able to persuade me to join her."

"Would it not be better were we to go to Lord Calthrope? Supposing he does not respond to your note, Aunt?" Arabella questioned anxiously.

"I will word the note in such a way that he will hardly dare refuse, and I will insist that my messenger await his answer."

"Oh, very good, your ladyship," Mr. Capell exclaimed.

"I am delighted that you, at least, approve, Mr. Capell." Lady Olivia smiled.

"I vow!" Lord Calthrope, a tall, handsome man in his early forties, dark like his nephew and bearing so strong a family resemblance to him that Arabella had had some difficulty in holding back her tears. "I will send Lane packing. He should have known better than to turn you away, my dear."

"My niece was rather travel-stained," Lady Olivia pointed out.

"All the same, he should know the difference between silk purses and sows' ears, and since it is evident that he does not, I shall not retain him in my employ. And you say that the lad has already been jailed for two days?"

"Yes, my lord." It was Mr. Capell who answered. "And held in solitary confinement."

"Damn the man!" Lord Calthrope frowned. "For a duel? That my nephew should have been rotting in that jail two minutes! And if I know Dorne . . ." He glanced at Arabella and then, frowning, continued, "I wish I did not know him and I hope he is suffering as much pain as he damn well deserves. He has lorded it or, rather, kinged it over that town far too long." He moved back and forth across the room. "We will return in my traveling coach. I will have the Gordons' post chaise, bless 'em, driven back by one of my people." He looked at Mr. Capell. "I have the feeling that time is of the essence. Dorne's a rogue under the best of circumstances, and a wounded rogue . . ." He looked at Arabella. "Can you be ready to travel by this afternoon?"

"We will be," Lady Olivia assured him. "I trust your traveling coach is large enough to accommodate three females?"

"Three, Aunt?" Arabella asked.

"Child, you must have a chaperon."

"But I am wed," she started to protest.

"Your aunt is quite right, my dear." Lord Calthrope bent an approving eye on Lady Olivia.

"And now that that is settled, I suggest that we be on the road by one at the latest. If"—he turned to Lady Olivia—"you can be ready by then?"

"Of course, my lord," she answered equably. "However, I think—"

"What now?" he cried and then reddened. "I beg your pardon, milady. What were you about to say?"

"I feel that I must dispatch a letter by messenger to my brother. There's no need to let him suffer longer nor his wife either. As I have told you, Arabella . . ." She paused, meeting her niece's worried and impatient look. "But enough, let us prepare for the journey."

"Please," Arabella cried, her frightened thoughts fixed only on her husband. Though she was quite sure that he had not intended to disturb her, she guessed that Lord Calthrope's decision to leave this very day was predicated on her husband's plight, which might be even more perilous than she had originally believed.

Indeed, it seemed to her that she had been holding her breath until she, her aunt, and Lizzie were ensconced in his lordship's commodious traveling coach. Byron insisted on driving the Gordons' post chaise back to Ipswich. Lord Calthrope, mounted on a huge chestnut stallion, was riding beside the equipage, which also had a number of outriders behind and before it. Yet, despite their presence and despite the luxurious interior of the well-sprung coach, Arabella could think only of Julian, held in jail. Lord Dorne was a power in that town and he had sole jurisdiction over the man at whose hands he had suffered a painful and ignominious defeat. She forbore to give her imagination full rein—she could only pray that their journey back to Ipswich would be as swift as it had been before.

A rainstorm complete with jagged flashes of lightning and deafening claps of thunder resulted in a stopover of a night and a day in Goldhanger, a town well known to Mr. Capell because of its theater. They stayed at the ancient Chequers Inn, Lord Calthrope requesting chambers for Mr. Capell, for Lady Olivia and her niece, and one for himself and Markham, his valet. The innkeeper was positively obsequious as he bowed the party inside, but there was no urging Arabella to partake of a particularly delicious meal. She lay in her chamber, her eyes fastened on the rain-streaked windows, dully watching the drops trickling unevenly down the windowpanes.

Lady Olivia had stayed beside her a little while, vainly trying to comfort her, but it soon became obvious that Arabella, so utterly changed from the lively girl she had known, wanted to be alone.

She had left Lord Calthrope and Mr. Capell in a small private dining room downstairs, and since his lordship had asked for news, she was returning there. On coming down the stairs, she found that the long hall, with its low beamed ceiling and oiled wood floors, was much darker than it had been when she had ascended the stairs with her niece.

A flash of lightning and a roll of thunder brought her to a momentary halt. Flurries of wind-driven rain splashed against the windows. She shook her head, wishing strongly that the weather would clear. Poor Arabella would be even more cast down were they forced to remain longer at the inn with her husband locked in jail. She sighed and continued down the stairs, her eyes on the door to the chamber where she had left Lord Calthrope and Mr. Capell, wondering now if they were still there. How long had she remained with her niece? There were so many things on her mind that she was not quite sure.

On reaching the foot of the stairs, Lady Olivia was about to go toward the dining room when a gentleman strolled out of the taproom and looking up, smiled broadly. Quickening his pace, he strode purposefully in her direction. He was a tall burly individual, well-dressed, but she was quickly aware that she had been wrong in characterizing him as a gentleman. No gentleman would look at her so boldly. His eyes were dark, almost black, and they wandered over her slender shape in a way that made her long to hit him. However, discretion being much the better part of valor in this instance, she turned away quickly and started for the stairs again, only to have him reach her side in what appeared to be a single stride.

Grinning insolently down at her, he put a hand on her arm, saying in a low, amused voice, "You're not leavin' us so soon, my lovely?"

Inwardly castigating herself for having come down into the main room when she might have known that her companions must have finished dinner, Lady Olivia neither looked at nor spoke to this importunate stranger. She tried to wrench her arm away, only to have his grip tighten, hurtfully.

"You will please release me, sir," she said freezingly.

"An' supposin' I do not want to release you," he demanded, his brandy-scented breath on her face. "Supposin' I want your company for a bit, my lady. You're a damned fine-lookin' woman, you are."

He was standing much too close to her and there

was a look in his eyes that frightened her. A hasty glance around the room showed her that though there were some men conversing, they were of a size that might make them unwilling to confront this oaf, were she to cry out. Indeed, he seemed to be growing taller by the minute, taller and extremely muscular, and his hard grip on her arm remained. She said, "I must ask you to stand aside, sir. I am going to my chamber."

He laughed. "And so am I. . . . What better way to wile away a rainy night. What do you say to French brandy, my love?"

"I say that you are sadly foxed, sir, and if you do not release me, I will scream."

"Ah." He chuckled. "There speaks a sly puss. Do you intend to raise your price by these subterfuges? Well, I'm game, but first let me have a taste of what is offered." He wrenched her toward him. Then, winding both arms around her slender shoulders, he brought his grinning mouth down on her lips.

However, in that same moment, he was roughly thrust aside, his arms pinioned behind his back, and then he was pushed across the hall to the front door of the inn. Unmindful of his struggles and his yells of rage, his captor thrust him into the pelting rain and disappeared with him, slamming the door behind him.

A shaken Lady Olivia, her hand to her assaulted mouth, found her legs suddenly giving way beneath her. She sank down on the stairs, thinking, but she was not sure what she was thinking, so swift had been her assailant's progress to the door! Furthermore, he had been escorted by Lord Calthrope, who had suddenly arisen from nowhere—or so it had seemed to her in her present confused state of mind.

That there were others in the hall who were similarly confused was evident by a babble of questions coupled with looks toward her and toward the door. Then, that portal was opened again and Lord Calthrope, his hair wet and plastered against his forehead and an extremely grim expression on his face, strode inside, slamming the door behind him. He did not stop to answer any of the questions directed of him. He came to where Lady Olivia still sat.

"My lady," he said breathlessly, "that savage will not trouble you again. I am very sorry that you were put through so shocking an experience. May I offer you a glass of wine and may I hope that you will forgive me?"

She regarded him confusedly. "You . . . you wish my forgiveness for *rescuing* me?"

He shook his head. "No, for having assumed you were acquainted with that lout. I saw you conversing with him, you see."

"He was conversing with me, sir. He came up to me just as I was about to go back upstairs." She shuddered. "I suggested to him that I was not desirous of his company, but he . . . " Her voice suddenly broke. "I am very glad that you finally realized we were not friends."

"Had his back not been to me, I should have guessed it immediately," Lord Calthrope grimaced. Then he frowned. "But, my dear Lady Olivia, why did you come down here alone?"

"I had expected to find you and—and Mr. Capell," she explained, wishing that she had not seemingly singled his lordship out. "I expect I had remained longer with my niece than I had realized."

"Yes, you were gone quite a while. I was sorry when you did not return, but I imagined your concern over the poor child must have held you at her side."

"It did, of course, and I would have stayed longer, but she really did not want me. She is in such distress."

"And might well be," he said soberly. "These jails . . . all jails are rat holes." He grimaced. "The thought of Julian being there an hour, much less the better part of a week . . . It is better not to dwell on it, but by God, I am tempted to finish what the boy began. It is my misfortune to have some slight acquaintance with Dorne. He is a bad man. And God help anyone who does him an injury, anyone who is not in a position to fend for himself." Lord Calthrope suddenly looked very grim. "If he has hurt my nephew in any way, he will answer for it, I can assure you."

She regarded him anxiously. "Is it your feeling that he might have so done?"

"I am in hopes that his condition is such that a few of his fangs will be drawn. But damn this delay!" Lord Calthrope's eyes were on the rain-splashed windows. "We must get Julian out of that hole. The poor lad's already had his fill of incarceration due to my damned priggish brother-in-law and his whelp of a son." His eyes widened. "Good God, Lady Olivia," he exclaimed explosively. "I am three kinds of a fool. I was so concerned over my nephew's plight that I actually forgot that Mark, his elder brother, met his end a month back . . . broke his neck in a steeplechase."

"Oh, how terrible!"

"Terrible, no. Good riddance, and Julian stands to inherit. He is now Lord Egerton."

"His father is—"

"The Earl of Montforde," Calthrope said with a frown. "And if you wish to know why the lad's an actor, I will give you his history, provided you will also let me give you a glass of wine to soothe you."

"You may, my lord," she responded quickly. "I am quite on fire with curiosity."

"And so am I." He smiled at her. "We must trade stories, I am thinking, since I believe I am not wrong in imagining that my nephew's bride is of a rank that is equal to his own?"

"You are not wrong, my lord," Lady Olivia said, experiencing the curious sensations she had not experienced since the age of seventeen when she had been deeply in love with the young man who disappeared at the same time he learned that she had no dowry.

"I think we will return to the private dining room, if you have no objection?"

"None, my lord," she assured him.

Calthrope's story, recounted first, was in essence much the same as that his nephew had told to her ladyship's niece, save that in place of Julian's shame was his uncle's indignation.

"If my sister had been alive, there'd have been no incentive for poor Julian to turn spendthrift. He would have been happy, for she loved him dearly, but she was not well after his birth. Indeed, within eight months she was dead and his father and his elder brother, aged five, were most sadly bereft. They blamed her death on the baby and they disliked him accordingly."

"But how unjust," Lady Olivia cried.

"Entirely, since Julian, as he has subsequently proved, was the pick of the litter. However, he was held in anathema by his father and brother and consequently he was sent off to school early. Generally, he went home with one or another boy, for he was never welcome in his own house. He had inherited some money from his mother's family—otherwise, he would have been hard put to maintain his household in London. He had left home early, well aware that he was no more welcome as a youth than he had been when he was little." Lord Calthrope frowned. "If only I had been in London . . . But I have always had a roving nature. I satisfied it by being attached to Wellington's forces in Spain and Portugal, and by the time I, as the sole heir of my estate on my father's sudden death, sold out two years ago, Julian was freed from prison and on the road.

"I caught up with him in some town and offered to help him, but he refused it." He grimaced. "The lad told me that he liked the work, but he was pleased to have my direction. He was a little indecisive about his future at the time. He was planning on marrying a dark-haired wench who was damned beautiful and supposedly born of reasonably good stock, but I did not believe her quite his equal."

"No, she was not," Lady Olivia said wryly.

"You know this young woman?" he asked interestedly.

"Yes, better than I have wished. Still, I must say that I like her rather more than I did when I first met her. In those days, the sun rose and set on her as far as my poor niece was concerned." Meeting his surprised gaze, she went on to match his story with her own, adding in conclusion. "The girl was quite amazingly distraught when she discovered that Arabella had fled."

"Why? She practically forced her from the house."

"I begin to believe that she is not very intelligent."

"My sentiments exactly, but please, continue."

"She insisted that Arabella was upset over her marriage to her father and was doing her utmost to come between them. She believed that my niece was trying to queen it over her, and she took exception to everything that she did. Of course, it is my opinion that she always resented Arabella's wealth and position and furthermore had felt diminished by the casual way in which she accepted her good fortune. Serena's life at home had been a matter of scrimping, saving, and living under the very real threat of Debtor's Prison. Yet, oddly enough, despite her strong resentment, I have the impression that Serena liked Arabella in her own peculiar way."

"Peculiar indeed," he commented, "insisting that she marry a man she hated."

"According to my brother, Serena thought Lord Kinnard an ideal husband for my niece. He is well-born, wealthy, and certainly eligible. She could not understand why Arabella did not agree with her. She has not the wit to see beneath the surface of an individual. To Serena, Lord Kinnard was all charm."

"I see," he gave her a thoughtful look, "but surely your brother knew his daughter's mind?"

Lady Olivia sighed. "My brother was often away while Arabella was growing up. Actually, he felt that Serena knew her better than he did, and since he was so much in love with the girl, it was very easy for her to persuade him that Arabella was lying to him. It is even possible that she believed it herself. It was a terrible shock to her when Arabella disappeared and a terrible shock to my brother as well. He put the Bow Street Runners on her trail, but she seemed to have disappeared into thin air. We were afraid that she had met with some fatal misadventure. Naturally, it caused quite a breach between my brother and his wife. They are more compatible now, mainly because Serena was so ill after Arabella's disappearance. I have not acquainted my niece with the whole story, but Serena had been expecting a child and lost it."

"Oh," he said. "I am sorry about that. It must have been a deep disappointment to your brother, as well."

"Yes. Furthermore, being miserable over Arabella's plight, he has been hard put to comfort her, feeling as he does that she is to blame for all that has happened."

"You are saying in effect that the marriage is at an end?"

"No, he still has a fondness for her, might love her. I think he does, but I do not believe that he will ever care for her as he first did. In those days he was blinded by passion."

"And now the blinders are removed. A pity," Lord Calthrope murmured. "It is unfortunate that she had none of the bravery displayed by your niece. It amazes me that Arabella, born to luxury, has been able to adapt herself so well to the life that wretched girl left behind."

"Arabella has always been in love with acting. She is a fine little actress—at least that is what I have deduced from her readings. Of course, I have never seen her on the professional stage."

"My nephew writes of her as if she were another Siddons." He frowned. "Damn and blast this delay. The wretch he wounded is going to make him suffer for every twinge of pain he inflicted! I can only hope that Dorne is too ill to do his worst."

"His worst?" she repeated anxiously. "He could not order an execution, could he?"

"No, he does not wield quite that much authority, not without a trial, but he could put him on slender rations and in some hole of a cell and in chains. But thank God, if I cannot buy him free, he can be tried by a jury of his peers and I might add that Lord Dorne is known as a despot and a despoiler of innocents. One wretched servant girl drowned herself. There was a stir about that. There will be a greater one now."

"Oh, God," Lady Olivia murmured. "Oh, for Mercury's winged sandals!"

"Indeed," he said gravely, his eyes lingering on her face. "And what is your story, milady?"

She met his eyes and was once more struck by his resemblance to his nephew. "It is not very interesting, my lord."

"I cannot believe that." He leaned forward. "It has to be interesting, even fascinating, since I see no wedding ring on your finger. I hope you are not mourning a lover killed in Portugal or Spain."

"Alas, 'tis nothing so romantic, my lord. Mine is the tale of a dowerless female who worked as a governess for some years while her brother was in India trying to retrieve the family fortunes. She kept house for him when he returned and helped bring up his motherless daughter."

"And that is all?" he demanded incredulously.

"Yes, my lord, all."

"Up until now." He smiled. "Your, er, future might prove entirely different."

Meeting his eyes, Lady Olivia experienced an odd, unfamiliar warmth stealing over her body, and she was uncomfortably aware that she was blushing. However, she said lightly, "Are you casting yourself in the role of a prognosticator, my lord?"

"I do not need to assume that mantle, my dear Lady Olivia, to assure you that life is full of surprises, and that a young woman in her prime, who is both well-born and beautiful, cannot hope to imagine that her future will prove to be a duplication of her past."

Her cheeks felt very hot, but Lady Olivia managed to reply with her usual calm, "You are kind to say so, my lord."

"No," he said thoughtfully. "I am not kind. I do not have a reputation for kindness, but I am known to be very honest and I dislike fulsome compliments. If one cannot speak the truth, it is better to say nothing. I have always lived by that belief." He gave her a long look. "But the hour grows late and we have, hopefully, a full day of traveling ahead of us. May I escort you to the door of your chamber? Or, rather, I *will* escort you there, for if I do not, you will surely encounter one or another importunate bumpkin and I will have to bruise my knuckles on his chin."

"You are most kind," Lady Olivia murmured.

He bent an irate eye upon her. "You will really have to cease from calling me 'kind.' If you must have a comparison, say that I am honest."

"Oh, I am quite sure that you are, my lord." She smiled and, rising, took his proffered arm.

He escorted her out of the chamber, across the floor, up the stairs, and stood waiting while she unlocked her chamber door and let herself inside.

"I will bid you good night, my lord," she said with something less than her usual sangfroid.

"I will wish you the same, my lady." He bowed over her hand and then said almost sternly, "I beg you will close the door and let me hear your key turn in the lock."

"Yes, my lord," she said obediently, and having obeyed him, she had no notion of the rather long time he stood there surveying the door with a smile of wonder and a burgeoning happiness on his face.

11

"Six days, six long days!" Arabella, clutching the strap that hung beside her, stared at buildings she remembered, those buildings that rose on the outskirts of Ipswich. Her thoughts flew to the crumbling jail where Julian lay incarcerated. It was near seven in the evening and a heavy fog hung whitely in the air. Seeing it, she shuddered, thinking of it seeping through the cracks and crevices of the cell where her husband had lain for almost a week.

"My dearest, do not anticipate the worst." Lady Olivia put her arm around her niece's tense shoulders, stifling an inward sigh. She was only too aware of the futility of her remarks, well aware, too, that it was late to be of any help to poor Julian at this hour. However, she held her peace and hoped against hope that she was in error.

Unfortunately, as she anticipated, it proved impossible to speak to the custodian of the jail so late at night, and a nearly prostrate Arabella was less persuaded than forced into bed at her lodgings, now so dingy and depressing without the vibrant and loving presence of her husband.

Mr. Capell, going to see the Gordons, returned with the equally depressing intelligence that they had been forbidden to see Julian, with the ominous suggestion that if his wounded lordship did not recover, they might all be considered culpable. He had imparted this dictum to Lord Calthrope, who subsequently conveyed the information to Lady Olivia.

"I think we will not acquaint my niece with that news," she told him. "The poor child is quite beside herself with worry. Perhaps in the morning you will be able to speak with someone in authority."

"I will that," he responded grimly. "I will speak to Dorne."

"Oh, I do wish I might go with you," she cried.

"And I am glad that you cannot. I am sure you are acquainted with the tales of wounded lions—think of Lord Dorne as a particularly heinous example of the species. However, it is possible that I may draw his teeth with a few well-chosen words."

"Oh, please," she cried, stretching out her hand.

He bore it to his lips, holding it a trifle longer than custom demanded. "I will do my best," he assured her, and releasing her hand, he bowed and left.

Lord Dorne's castle lay at the outskirts of the city in a vast park. An imposing edifice of gray stone, it had stood there for over five hundred years, its square towers rising starkly over the surrounding trees.

Lord Calthrope, being driven toward it, leaned out of the window of his post chaise and thought that its gray outlines under the weak glow of a cloud-shrouded morning sun expressed its owner's grim personality most vividly.

He drew and expelled a long, hissing breath. He had been at the jail earlier that morning and had been denied access to the prisoner by a constable who had spoken to him with an insolence that had made him long to respond with a strong blow to the man's ugly face. He was still seething with the frustration he had experienced upon being unable to do as all his senses save one dictated. However, that one, common sense, told him he had acted wisely, and adjured him to continue acting in that same cautious vein.

Consequently, upon meeting a gatekeeper no more prepossessing than the constable, he managed to keep his burgeoning anger well-concealed as he smoothly informed the man of his great regard for his stricken employer. He reinforced those sentiments with a gold piece, which, he suspected, was the key that opened the gates. He had no difficulty gaining admittance to the house, since the butler, who also presided over Lord Dorne's London establishment, knew him, even though he was not a frequent visitor there.

"I am told that your master is gravely ill," Lord Calthrope began.

"He has been hurt, my lord, but—" the butler began and was interrupted by his lordship himself, who came stomping in, looking pale but entirely able to walk.

"Ah, good morning, Athol," Lord Calthrope said genially. "I see that your health is much improved. And here I was led to believe that you were within inches of death's door."

Lord Dorne stared at his visitor with a consternation that was almost immediately supplanted by a frown. "Calthrope," he rasped, "what would you be doing in these parts? Sure you have not come to pay *me* a visit?"

"In a manner of speaking, Athol, that is precisely why I have come," his visitor said coolly. "I am here on behalf of my nephew, Lord Egerton."

"Egerton?" His lordship frowned. "Did I not hear that he had recently died?"

"You did, Athol, my elder nephew came to an unfortunate end in the course of a steeplechase, and naturally, his younger brother came into the title and stands to inherit the earldom upon the eventual demise of his father. I am speaking of Julian Sherlay, whose wife you attempted to seduce."

Lord Dorne's mouth fell open and was closed instantly with a click of teeth that Lord Calthrope heard. He paused then gasped, "You . . . I . . ."

"Pray let me continue, Athol. The poor lad is, as I understand it, held incommunicado. He has been allowed no visitors and may not be released on bail— a damned peculiar state of affairs, considering that it was a duel and not a wanton attack on your august person."

"He . . . I . . ." Lord Dorne stuttered.

"As I was about to say, Athol," Lord Calthrope continued smoothly, "it is Julian's right, as I believe you must understand, to be tried by a jury of his peers, and if the evidence of such witnesses with whom I have already spoken is aired, your reputation will be even more odoriferous than it is at present. There are some members of the peerage who will not receive you now, but if you persist in this farce, I can assure you that the Prince Regent, who on occasion has been pleased to find you amusing, will give you the cut direct. I, too, enjoy his highness's friendship and will give him a full account of your, er, activities. I need not mention, I am sure, that in the face of the Prince's dissatisfaction, London will be the richer for your absence. Unless, of course, you see reason and drop the charges against my nephew."

"Damn you to hell," Lord Dorne burst out, his face flushed and contorted by rage.

"Is that your answer, then, Athol?" Lord Calthrope asked lightly. "Very well, I will start proceedings."

"Hold, damn you," Lord Dorne rasped. "How was I to know that an actor, a damned actor . . . Why did he say nothing?"

"The news of his brother's demise had not yet reached him. Will you give me a note for the jailer, Athol?"

"And how is it that a peer of the realm is wed to a little slut who—"

"That little slut, as you are pleased to call her," Lord Calthrope interrupted, "is Lady Arabella Ashmore. Her father, Lord Ashmore . . ." He paused, staring at Lord Dorne's flushed face. "If you do not wish an attack of apoplexy, I think you must try to get control of your temper."

Lord Dorne took several long breaths before saying in a constricted voice, "Will you let this story get around?"

"The story concerning your attempted seduction of Lady Arabella and your unlawful imprisonment of his lordship?" Lord Calthrope demanded coldly. "No, not if you will call off your dogs—that is to say, exonerate my nephew of any wrongdoing and admit that it was you who forced the duel on him by your actions with his wife. Since you are the justice of the peace, I think you may successfully appeal to his worship that he grant my nephew a full pardon—the writ, witnessed by me and your butler in the library in this house. I would like the said justice to empower me to have my nephew released. If the said justice of the peace will do as I ask, I do not imagine that the

Prince will hear about this particular episode."
Meeting his lordship's fury-filled gaze, he added
coolly, "Well, Athol, what is your answer?"

"Come to the library, damn you, and you shall
have your writ," Dorne growled.

Confronted by a chill-faced Lord Calthrope and a
pale, furious Lord Dorne, enjoined to be present
mainly because Lord Calthrope had not quite trusted
his epistle and thought him capable of rescinding it
with a hastily delivered message, the constable also
paled.

"I am to r-release the ac-actor?" he stuttered.

"Aye, bring him out, I say. He is free to go."

"F-free, yer lordship?" the constable almost
wailed.

"Aye, as I have said. I have dropped all charges
against him. Fetch him at once," Lord Dorne
snapped.

Lord Calthrope, listening to an exchange he found
singularly sinister, fastened cold eyes on Lord Dorne,
saying brusquely, "If my nephew has sustained any
injury while in the hands of your creatures, here—"

"I did not call for torture," Lord Dorne retorted,
though considerably less belligerently than before.
"He will come on his own two feet, I assure you." He
glared at the constable and at the jailer, who had just
joined him. "Why are you standing there? Do as I
say!"

"Yes, your lordship," the constable responded
weakly. He turned to the jailer, adding, "Go on,
man, do as his lordship says." Then, meeting the
latter's concerned glance, he added, "I'll be going
down with you."

"Down is it?" Lord Calthrope turned on Lord Dorne. "In a dungeon, then?"

"Our facilities up here are for misdemeanors," Lord Dorne said weakly, and failed to meet his companion's fiery glance.

It was some little time before the men returned, and in the interim Lord Calthrope found himself holding his breath as he took in the battered appearance of even the outer areas of the jail. He could imagine the dark, dismal cells that lay below and remembered Julian's pain as he had described his sojourn in the King's Bench Prison, he himself being out of the country at the time and unaware of his nephew's ordeal. Had he known, he would have gladly paid his debts. But compared to the quarters here, the King's Bench was a veritable hotel! And Julian had been held in this wretched place for six days—six days and seven nights at the mercy of Dorne, whose orders he did not like to contemplate.

Then, suddenly, they were back, the jailer and the constable. Between them, they supported a lean young man in a dirty shirt and trousers, his face covered with a week's beard. He was walking, but slowly, very slowly, and as he came closer, Lord Calthrope winced at the fetid odor that arose from him while Lord Dorne hastily put his handkerchief to his nose.

"Damn you to hell, Athol," Lord Calthrope said distinctly, and coming forward, he put his arm around his nephew's thin shoulders.

"Lad," he said huskily, "you are free."

Julian stared dully at him out of deeply circled eyes. "Arabella," he whispered. "They said that she has been taken to Dorne's house."

"Whoever told you that lied through his damned

teeth," Lord Calthrope said angrily. "Arabella is safe. She is with her aunt in your lodgings, my lad. You must come with me to the White Horse and get cleaned up, I think. And how long is it since you have eaten?"

Julian did not appear to have heard him. "They said that he . . . that she . . ."

"No, lad, your wife is unhurt. I swear it."

"She was not r-ravished or . . . or . . ."

"No, lad," Lord Calthrope said, making a strong effort to swallow his rage. "Your wife came to London to fetch me. She returned last night." Then, with an exclamation of shock, he caught his fainting nephew in his arms. With a long cold look at Lord Dorne, he said as he hoisted Julian over his shoulder, "You told me, damn you to hell, that you did not use torture." Without waiting for a response, Lord Calthrope strode outside, and with the help of his horrified postboy and coachman, he eased Julian into the waiting post chaise. Climbing in beside him, he rasped, "The White Horse Inn."

As she had been for the last fortnight, Arabella was ill in the morning, but it had yet taken all of Lady Olivia's powers of persuasion to keep her from going to the jail. However, finally, reluctantly, she had yielded to her aunt's entreaties, and weary from the hectic journey, her condition, and her anguish over Julian's plight, she had fallen asleep while her aunt watched over her, wondering futilely why she had heard nothing from Lord Calthrope and hoping against hope that her niece would not wake before there was news of her husband.

Despite her faith in his lordship, Lady Olivia could not help but feel singularly distressed as the little

battered clock on the mantelshelf inexorably ticked
the minutes away, chiming out nine, then ten, then
eleven crystalline notes, while she sat in her chair
trying to quell her anxiety by reading. She had
acquired the novel in London and it was highly
touted by the critics, but though she read words and
turned pages, she did not really know what she had
been perusing. Then, finally, when the hands of that
clock pointed to ten minutes before the hour of
twelve, there was a knock on the door of the outer
room. Hurrying to open it, she found Lord Calthrope
with a slender young man whom she barely
recognized as Julian Sherlay, so pale and wan did he
look.

"My wife?" he said without preamble, anxiety in
his tone and in his eyes.

"She is sleeping—" Lady Olivia began as she
stepped back to allow him to enter.

"No, no, she is not," cried a voice behind her.
"Oh, Julian, Julian, Julian!" Arabella came forward,
and as Lady Olivia hastily stepped aside, she threw
her arms around her husband, to be held against him
while he murmured little broken words of love, to
which she responded most joyfully in kind.

Moving hurriedly through the doorway, Lady
Olivia stepped into the hall and joined Lord Calthrope, who still stood there. She wanted to thank
him, but much to her consternation, she found she
could not speak. She could only look up at him, the
tears running down her cheeks while he, putting a
strong, sustaining arm around her waist, led her
down the narrrow steps of the lodging house and
without an argument from her, helped her into his
waiting post chaise and commanded his coachman to
be off.

* * *

Inside their chamber, seeing Julian's frailty and weakness, Arabella made him lie down on the bed and, ignoring his protests, gently removed his garments, urging him to lie back on the pillows. Sliding down beside him, she cradled him in her arms as if he were her child.

Neither spoke. They held each other wordlessly and, as always when they were together, gave strength to each other so that finally she could tell him the news that she had intended to break to him on the night that had begun so beautifully and that had ended in such terror.

She lay with her lips pressed against his cheek, rejoicing now in the safety she had willingly surrendered for him and now willingly resumed for him. She was ready to cast aside all the aspirations that, she realized now, meant nothing to her, not without the only person in the world whose applause she wanted to hear.

"My love," she said gently but joyfully, "I am going to have your child, our child." And now she looked at him with just a touch of apprehension lest he not wish to relinquish this life of peril, yet great rewards.

He was silent so long that her apprehension was growing stronger, but as a question trembled on her lips, it was forced back by his long kiss.

"Oh, my love, my very dearest." Julian kissed her again and there was no doubting the happiness mirrored in his dark eyes. Then, he fell silent again, unable to fend off a long and much-needed sleep in which she joined him presently, for she was truly weary from pretending to that same sleep for the three hours that ended with his arrival.

As she said later, over dinner with her husband, her aunt, her uncle-by-marriage, and also Byron Capell, "You did believe me asleep, Aunt Olivia, I know you did. This morning, I mean."

"And you were not?" Lady Olivia asked confusedly.

"I was not," Arabella said. "How could I sleep not knowing what had happened to Julian?" She gave her husband a loving smile. "I was in utter, utter agony as the clock ticked the minutes away and the minutes became hours, but I could not burden you with my anxiety and so I pretended to sleep. It was quite the best bit of acting I have ever done and there was no one to recognize it."

Then she laughed delightedly as those around the table startled the other patrons in the dining room with a great burst of enthusiastic if necessarily belated applause.

Epilogue

Toward ten in the evening of a summer night and under a sky filled with stars and a moon that seemed preternaturally bright, a performance of *The Taming of the Shrew* had just ended. Standing on a platform set up in the middle of a vast garden bordered by a lake, the actors were bowing. At first, it seemed as if a small but extremely enthusiastic audience would not let them go.

"*Bis, bis . . .*" a gentleman called. "That is how they ask for repeats in Italy and then get them. Let us hear Kate's speech again." Jumping to his feet, he clapped even louder.

"I beg you will sit down," his wife protested laughingly.

He obeyed immediately, leaning over to whisper, "It's a shame. They are both so gifted, far too gifted for these amateur performances, Olivia. They need scenery."

"There is nothing amateur about them," Lady Olivia said. "*They* are professional and so are the other actors. They are all from the Gordon's company. Do not forget that Shakespeare's plays were acted on a bare platform stage, too, and they do have costumes and they have an audience, larger than last year, too. A great many of the local gentry are here.

You would not want them to go out on the road again, subject to the attentions of men like the late Lord Dorne?''

''You are right, as usual, my love. Let us go back and see them, shall we?''

''Let us wait until they come out,'' she said.

He smiled down at her. ''We seem at cross purposes this evening, my dear Olivia. Will you still argue with me if I suggest that we walk about the garden and mourn the fact that Capability Brown was dead before he could design our gardens?''

''Oh, I do not mourn that. I think our gardens are exactly what I like and the children certainly love them. But,'' she rose, ''I would appreciate a little walk with you.''

He rose and reaching down pulled her up. ''Ah, acquiescence at last,'' he murmured, as they skirted the audience and moved toward the late Mr. Brown's artfully designed lake.

Meanwhile, in a small dressing room Arabella removed her red wig and Julian winced as he pulled off his bristling mustache, while the Bianca, a member of the Gordon players, combed her fair hair and looked admiringly at her fellow actors.

''You are every bit as good as my parents have said,'' she commented. ''You ought to go on the road with us. My father and mother have never ceased to mourn your Romeo and Juliet, especially now that Mama cannot possibly play Juliet any more.''

''Come, come, Nancy,'' Arabella said, laughing at this backhanded compliment. ''This theater must needs suffice as our road.''

''It is a rare waste,'' the girl said positively. ''Though I suppose you being . . .'' She hesitated and blushed. ''Oh my, I do beg your pardon, my lord and your ladyship. I'd fallen into believing you was real actors.''

Arabella and Julian burst into delighted laughter.

"And so we are,'' Julian affirmed. "Have you not heard that all the world's a stage, my child?''

"I expect it can be,'' Nancy Gordon said nervously, "but still it's a pity you are no longer in the profession.''

"But, I repeat, we are,'' Julian assured her. "As long as there is this stage we have set up and 'tis midsummer night's eve—when the fairies are abroad and will grant us our wishes for a night. Come, it's time we joined our audience.''

Nancy hung back. "You go first,'' she said. "It is you they want to see.''

"We will go together, Madame Bianca,'' Arabella said firmly. As they came out of the dressing room, she and Julian put Nancy between them, and linking arms with her, they walked past the now empty seats to a clearing in which stood a long table loaded with fruits, cakes, candies and wine. The other performers and some thirty guests were milling around the table, but as soon as the trio of actors appeared, they broke into cheers and sustained applause, after which Lord Ashmore embraced Arabella and said warmly, "That was a notable performance, my dearest.'' He had a warm smile for Julian, as well. "There were times when I was ready to rush up on stage and protect my daughter from you. You perform the role of a bully with remarkable insight. I hope it does not trickle off into real life?''

"Ask your daughter to display her bruises and her bites for your edification, sir.'' His son-in-law laughed.

"Bruises and bites, Julian, fie, I cannot believe it,''

said the slender woman at Lord Ashmore's side. She
turned to Arabella. "That does bring back memories
of our thespian exercises at school, my dear."

Arabella said easily, "I thought it must, Serena,
even though I played Petruchio in those days."

"And I was Kate. Gracious, it does seem such a
very long time ago. And I have the gray hair to prove
it." Serena pointed to her coronet of braids, now
liberally sprinkled with silver.

"Your hair looks beautiful, Serena," Arabella
commented.

"Does it? I do not believe your father agrees. He
used to tell me that my midnight locks made me look
like an houri from the Garden of Paradise." Serena
looked up at her husband. "Do you remember that,
Adrian?"

He had been staring into darkness. "I beg your
pardon, my love. What did you say?" He looked
questioningly at Serena.

"Nothing, really." She shrugged and turned back
to Arabella. "You were within your rights when you
introduced me as your mother earlier this evening. I
expect I do look much older since my illness."

"Nonsense, my dear Serena." Lord Ashmore's
smile was forced this time. "You look entirely
beautiful. Lord Colvine was remarking on that just
the other day."

"Oh, was he?" She looked up at him provocatively. "I hope you were not jealous."

"Not in the least, my dear."

"But I *want* you to be jealous," she said with a tiny
pout.

"Do you, my sweet? Then I promise to be in a
jealous rage the next time anyone pays my lovely
wife a compliment. Does that satisfy you?"

"You do think I am lovely?"

"Of course, my dear," he responded obediently.

"An houri from the garden of paradise?" she pursued.

"Quite, my dear."

"That is nice. And you are not angry anymore?"

"Of course not, my dear, what put that into your head?"

"I do not like it when you are angry. Where are the children?"

"You sent them to bed, my dear."

"Did I? I must look in on them. Three such darlings. They will want me and I will take some sweetmeats to them?"

"They will like that, my dear," Lord Ashmore said gently.

"Yes, I think they will." She moved to the table and after a moment, her husband nodding to his daughter and his son-in-law, followed her. Catching up with her, he put his arm around her waist and together they selected sweetmeats from the table.

"Oh, dear," Arabella sighed. "For a moment, she seemed more like the old Serena. She was actually flirting with him. Then, that odd change came over her. You told me that people do recover from a . . . crisis of the nerves, is that not what you called it?"

"Yes, a crisis of the nerves," Julian affirmed. "I once knew an actor who was similarly afflicted and that is how his physician described it. People do recover from it. I think Serena is much better than she was when last we saw her."

"Yes, I think you are right. And she is a good mother. She adores those children." Arabella frowned. "I do wish Papa were a little more interested in her."

"She forfeited his interest, my dear," Julian said coolly.

"We have agreed that she was very uncertain, very ill at ease in her new life."

"Yes, we have agreed on that and so has he, but still she revealed some character traits he cannot admire. He, alas, is not the first to discover that beauty without a lively intelligence is a rather worthless possession."

"Ah, and here you are, my Kate and Petruchio!" Lady Olivia, followed by her husband, came to her niece's side. "I am deeply, abjectly sorry for the noise our son made in the midst of your first scene. He is teething and very fretful. Your nurse said that I should have left him in the nursery with Serena's brood and she was right, but . . ."

"But"—Julian fastened a mischievous look on his uncle's face—"his father would not countenance it, and after all, your son and heir did quiet down."

"Due to the fact that I had my hand over his mouth," Lord Calthrope grinned.

"You are fortunate the child did not bite you," his nephew commented. "Our Juliet, if you can imagine, has been known to do that very thing."

Lord Calthrope laughed. "Your daughter bids fair to being a limb, as our nurse says. As for Hugh Julian Robert Alexander, named for an uncle, a nephew, a father, and a Macedonian general, he did try to bite me, but fortunately his teeth number two and they are both on top. Where, by the way, are my great-nephew and my great-niece?"

"They are reposing in the nursery. We hope they are sleeping. Little James might be but I suspect that Juliet is not. They were so active earlier in the evening that Lizzie insisted they go to bed, and she is right.

They are at an age where they are into everything, not excluding the lake." Arabella rolled her eyes. Turning to her aunt, she added, "Serena is looking better, do you not agree?"

"Yes, I do. She seems brighter, too. Of course, she is always happier when Adrian is home," Lady Olivia commented.

"Yes," Arabella acknowledged. "He told me that he does not believe he will return to India soon again."

"He always says that," Lady Olivia sighed. "I hope that the poor girl has no inkling of the real reason he travels to India and stays so long."

"I fear, or, rather, I hope, that she has not the acumen to realize that, er, dark-eyed houris are indigenous to India's fabled shores." Julian grimaced.

"Perhaps he does mean it when he says he does not intend to return to India," Arabella said. "It is a very long journey and he is fond of the children. Arthur is a delightful little boy and he will inherit the title. Serena is good with the children, too. She does not play favorites or coddle Baby Louise more than Tommy or Arthur. And even when she is not at her best, she plays with them just as if she were a child herself. I fear she did not have a very happy childhood." A distressed look came into her eyes. "Oh, dear, I ought to have guessed how very unsure she was of herself all those years ago. I sometimes believe her condition is partially my fault."

"Nothing is your fault, my love." Julian put his arm around his wife's slender waist. "Serena's breakdown was caused by herself and she *is* getting better and do let us stop worrying about her, my sweetest girl." He looked at his uncle and Lady Olivia. "Will you excuse us, please?"

"Of course," they chorused.

"Come, then," Julian murmured.

"Am I to know where we are going?" Arabella questioned.

"To the lake, of course, and then you will kiss me again, my Kate. Or should I have said, will you?"

"I certainly will, Petruchio. And is it not a lovely evening?"

"Entirely lovely, beautiful and exquisite," he agreed, his eyes lingering on her face. Then, he added, "Well, what says my own true love?"

"Your own true love says . . . do let us hurry and get nearer the shores of the lake before anyone else finds us and engages us in congratulatory conversation."

"A most excellent idea."

Arm in arm, they ran down the slope to the lake, dark under the night sky and with the full moon serenely floating on its water. They moved nearer to a clump of trees and came to a stop.

"Well?" Julian asked.

"Your own true love says that, yes, from time to time I do miss the stage and wish that I might be merely a 'poor player,' who 'struts and frets his hour upon the stage . . .' Do not you?"

"From time to time," he admitted. "And this, of course, is one of those times. But . . ." He looked back over his shoulder seeing in his mind's eye, the great house rising behind them.

"Exactly," his wife agreed, needing no interpretation of that long backward look. She moved closer to him and wordlessly they embraced, their moon-cast shadows reflected in the wind-rippled waters of their lake. Then, hand in hand, they moved up the slope to attend to the needs of their audience.